M000041217

She looked at him with tear-filled eyes, and Oliver made the biggest mistake in his life. Pulling her close to him, he said tenderly, "I care a great deal more than that, Anne. I love you, my dear, and want to marry you."

"No! no!" she cried, tearing herself from his grasp. "I hate you; you are a Rowley like him. I will never marry you; you can't make me. I will never marry anyone."

She fled from the room and up the staircase, leaving Oliver to curse the fate that made him declare himself too soon. . . .

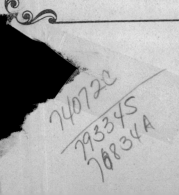

74072C
79334S
76834A

ANNE KEYWORTH

SPRING BRIDE

FAWCETT CREST • NEW YORK

A Fawcett Crest Book
Published by Ballantine Books

Copyright © 1982 by Anne Keyworth
First published in Great Britain 1982

All rights reserved under International and Pan-American Copyright
Conventions. Published in the United States by Ballantine Books, a
division of Random House, Inc., New York, and simultaneously in
Canada by Random House of Canada Limited, Toronto.

ISBN 0-449-21154-1

This edition published by arrangement with Robert Hale, Ltd.

Manufactured in the United States of America

First Ballantine Books Edition: October 1986

ONE

As the hired carriage turned in at the ornate gilded gates the driver was momentarily surprised at the grandeur before his eyes. A vast and well cared for park stretched as far as he could see in all directions and as no house was visible between the trees as yet, he guessed that the drive must be all of three miles long. To his left the park swept impressively down to a large lake some two miles distant and beyond the lake a densely wooded hill rose to be capped at its peak by a large tower-like folly. Turning to his right he saw more parkland dotted about with sheep, and crossed by a small winding river. On the other bank amongst the well tended trees a herd of red deer grazed peacefully. This was obviously the home of a gentleman of vast wealth, and he could think of no reason why the party in his carriage, who was equally obviously indigent, should have business in this establishment.

The party in the hired carriage was feeling no less surprised than the driver. Robin had told her that his cousin was wealthy but this grandeur was totally unexpected and rather intimidating. When the house at last came into view it took her breath away by its sheer size. The terraces and formal gardens laid out around it were dotted here and there with classical statues and the sweep of steps up to the imposing portico, supported on either side no less than four gryphons. Had she not been desperate Anne Rowley might well have told the driver to turn about and take her back to Cheltenham. She was however acutely aware of exactly how little money she had left and so her need overcame her fear. The driver stopped the horses and got down to open the door and let down the step for her. In the midst of all this grandeur he thought she looked even more shabby than before.

"Wait here for me please", she said resolutely. "I shan't be above fifteen minutes in all".

He watched with interest as she mounted the steps and rang the bell. The door was opened by a butler of such magnificence that the driver was glad he had not rung for admission.

"Yes", the butler intoned majestically, taking in the slight figure before him. He was aware that she was young and shabby, but years of sheltering his master from encroaching persons had taught him great perception. He was able to tell therefore that, although old, her clothes had been both fashionable and expensive.

"I would like to speak to Lord Welham for a few moments only", she said a little breathlessly, "If he is not available at the moment I am prepared to wait until such time as he will see me".

Porter, the butler, was gratified to learn that his first assessment had been correct, as her speech and manner indicated to him an undoubted lady of quality.

He said however, "His lordship does not see anyone without an appointment. He is an extremely busy man". He prepared to shut the door but was arrested by the lady's next words.

"I think he will see me however. Just tell him it is Mrs. Rowley". Her words had a profound effect on that majestic gentleman, and to the considerable surprise of the driver he opened the door wide and ushered her in.

The main hall of Welham Abbey was vast and very old. It was indeed the oldest part of the Abbey, which had grown in magnificence around it during the centuries. The whole was panelled in oak and hung about with many shields, weapons and armour of a bygone day. There were several portraits of past Rowley's who had enjoyed a successful military career in almost every war since the thirteenth century. The fine old oak staircase rose from the centre of the hall and divided into two halfway up. Anne Rowley looked around in some trepidation but nonetheless did not fail to notice that several of the rugs on the stone floor were badly in need of cleaning, and that a beautiful oval table sported a very sad bunch of flowers in a dull pewter bowl that had not seen water for many a day. Porter left her in the hall and crossed to a pair of double doors at the back on the left. He knocked, opened them and entered.

The library at Welham Abbey was Lord Welham's pride and joy. Those of the Rowley's who had not taken up a military career had all pursued scholastic learning and the present Earl was no exception. The pleasant L-shaped room possessed five large windows that looked out over the back terrace and formal gardens to the lake. Lord Welham however was not enjoying the view but pouring over a great quantity of papers on his desk in the centre of the room. He looked up irritably as Porter entered and said dryly, ''I had hoped that when I asked not to be disturbed this morning you would see to it that I was not. I heard the bell and expected that you would have sent any visitor away''.

Porter remained unperturbed by this and answered, ''I am aware that your lordship wished to remain undisturbed, but when I learned the name of your caller I made sure you would wish to see her''.

"Her!" His lordship said temporarily diverted, "It's not my Aunt is it?"

"No, my lord. It is a very young lady who claims to be Mrs. Rowley".

The effect on Lord Welham, of this name, was no less spectacular than it had been on Porter himself. He leapt to his feet and came around to the front of his desk. "Robin's wife, here," he said astounded. "Did she say why she had come?"

"Only to speak to you, my lord, it seems". Porter added a trifle frostily, "She has come in a dubious hired carriage which appears to be waiting for her".

"Has she indeed," said his lordship thoughtfully, "When you have shown her in pay off the carriage and send it away".

"Very good, my lord", said Porter and departed.

When Anne Rowley entered the library a few moments later she was met by a tall and extremely elegant man who she judged to be about thirty or thereabouts. He was dressed in riding clothes but of such elegance and style that they would have graced any drawing-room. He led her to a chair beside the fire, and she surreptitiously studied his face as she walked beside him. To call him handsome would not be correct she decided, but he was a very arresting man. His black hair was cut short à-la-brutus, his eyes, almost black, were hard and belied the smile on his well formed mouth, but his eyebrows, just now raised quizzically at her, had been drawn together and down at the instant of her entry and had given him an almost cruel look. From the lines on his face she guessed that life had not passed him by, and from his obvious arrogance mixed with charm she drew her own conclusions.

Lord Welham looked down at the slight figure walking beside him across the room, in her once elegant, but now shabby pelisse and thrice trimmed, out-moded bonnet. Although he knew that she was nearly twenty he could hardly believe it. She had an indifferent figure, though his lordship, a connoisseur of ladies, figures, suspected from the hang of her pelisse that she had once been fuller than she was now. Her face was ordinary, her hair scraped back and hardly visible, only her eyes when she looked at him held any life. His lordship wondered what it was that his handsome, charming cousin had seen in this dab of a girl to make him marry her out of hand and carry her off to Spain. Although Robin had been dead for a year now it still gave Lord Welham a pang to think of his cousin, whom he had loved, and this made his opening remark rather sharper than he had intended it to be.

"Why have you come?" To his amazement the slip of a girl in front of him was transformed into a spirited adversary by his words.

"Since you commanded me to do so a year ago, I am surprised that you should be so angry now that I have".

"But you did not come a year ago", he replied with equal spirit, "and after looking for you for nine months I had given you up for lost. Where have you been?"

"Why were you looking for me?", she asked heatedly, "It should have been obvious when I didn't answer your dictatorial letter that I had no wish to see you".

"But you are here now", he replied smoothly, "Why?"

She was angry with herself instantly for having allowed herself to become roused by his lordship, but his officious letter had rankled her for a long time. She looked down at her hands and composed herself before speaking.

"I have come to ask you if you will please help me in a scheme that I have evolved". She looked up to gauge his reaction and was dismayed to see him leaning negligently on the mantlepiece and regarding her with a sceptical smile. She looked down again hastily and continued, "You may not know that my father died shortly after I left England.

These past twelve months I have been living with my old Nurse in Ch . . . never mind where, suffice it to say that with her small annuity she cannot keep me indefinitely, although she says she can. I am desirous of setting myself up in a millinery shop and I have found the very place. However I need two hundred pounds to secure the property and buy stock. I have come to ask you if you will grant me a loan''.

"No!" said his lordship promptly.

"But I can repay you in three years easily. I have worked it all out and I am very good at decorating hats. I used to do all my Mama's'', she finished defensively.

"No!" said his lordship again.

She rose with a resolution she was far from feeling and said "I will bid you good-day then, my lord. Since you won't help me there is nothing more to say''.

She made for the door with dignity but his lordship was before her and said grimly, "There is a great deal more to say Mrs. Rowley. I was the executor of Robin's will and I wish to know exactly what happened to all of his money. I did not seek you for nine months for no reason''. He was surprised to see a look of fear on her face as she answered unsteadily.

"I have no idea where Robin's money went, my lord, so I am unable to help you. Please step out of the way and allow me to leave''.

"You are going nowhere until I have learned a great deal more of the two years you spent as Robin's wife''. He took her arm as he spoke and led her back to her chair.

"I have a carriage waiting,'' she said looking up at him. "I really must go; Nanny will wonder what has become of me. I can tell you nothing'', she added. "Nothing. Please let me go, my lord''.

The entreaty in her eyes was a little unnerving to his lordship, but he steeled himself and said, "The carriage has been sent away. I will have answers, Mrs. Rowley, so pray do not think that you can fob me off. Robin was my heir. I know every detail of his inheritance and I wish to know when and why Cuckfield was sold''.

She jumped to her feet and disregarding his questions said heatedly, ''How dare you send my carriage away. However will I get another one now? Nanny will be frantic with worry, I had to put up for the night last night because the wheel came off the carriage. I promised her I would be home by noon today. You hateful arrogant man'', she shouted at him and ran for the door.

Once again his lordship was there before her. He stood with his back to the door and said icily, ''Kindly comport yourself with dignity, Mrs. Rowley, and return to your seat''.

Beside herself with anger, desperation and fear Anne Rowley tried to push Lord Welham aside. He in his turn, angry that this young girl should evade his questions, grabbed her by the arms and shook her. Her eyes opened very wide, and she put up her hands defensively in front of her face. His lordship, annoyed at her defensive action pulled her hands down and surprised a look of sheer terror on her face before she swooned away. He caught her adroitly as she fell, and carried her to a sofa where he laid her down with a cushion behind her head. Her bonnet had slipped off so he untied the ribbons to remove it. Her hair, free from its restraint, fell in soft chestnut curls around her pale child's face and afforded his lordship a partial glimpse of the girl that Robin had married. He got up abruptly, rang the bell, then returned and unbuttoned and removed her pelisse. Then putting his hand on her heart found to his relief that it was beating slowly but firmly. The door opened to admit Porter. He showed neither surprise nor dismay at the scene that met his eyes but merely said,

''You rang, my lord''.

"Yes, Porter. As you see Mrs. Rowley has swooned, mainly from lack of food I think. Go down to the kitchen and procure some broth, some bread and a glass of milk. Bring them back yourself".

"Yes, my lord".

"Oh, and Porter, take Mrs. Rowley's things and put them in the Green Room".

A few moments later she opened her eyes slowly then shut them again. The face above her was not one that she wanted to see. His lordship spoke and his voice was gentle,

"How do you feel, child?"

She opened her eyes again and looked uncertainly up at him. He was seated on the sofa, and had one hand on either side of her. He smiled encouragingly.

"Did I swoon?" she asked interestedly, "I have never done so before".

"You did indeed and from lack of food if I am not mistaken".

He rose and went to a side table. She heard liquid being poured and realised how thirsty she was. When he came back with a glass of wine however she refused it.

"Nonsense," he said briskly putting his arm under her shoulders to raise her. "I don't myself like to see a lady drinking a great deal but this is only Madeira and will help to revive you." He put the glass to her lips as he spoke and to her surprise she found herself drinking. He lowered her back to the pillow and putting the glass down resumed his seat beside her. When he spoke again it was softly, but under the soft tone she detected a firmness,

"Mrs. Rowley, I would indeed be a fool to think that you had any of Robin's money or have had in a very long time, if the style of your dress is anything to go by. Nonetheless whilst I have no desire to upset you again, you must own that some answers are due to me. I loved Robin like a brother and his death at Waterloo was a terrible blow to me. Equally the state of his finances gave me a severe shock. If you will only speak to me about your time in Spain it may explain some of it to me.''

Before she could answer the door opened to admit Porter again. He was carrying a large silver tray covered with a spotless white napkin. He put it on a small table and when his lordship indicated, carried it over and placed it beside the chair by the fire. His lordship raised her up and helped her to the chair, then placed the small table before her and lifted the napkin.

The aroma of chicken broth assailed her and his lordship, with a smile said, ''Please eat, Mrs. Rowley. I'll not disturb you until you are quite finished.'' He strode over to his desk and commenced to examine some papers. Mrs. Rowley fell to with a will and silence came to the library.

The light meal was of great help to Anne for not only did it feed her, it also gave her time to think. She was aware that in spite of his lordship's soft tone he was determined to get answers. She was equally determined that he should get less than the truth. One reason was her fervent desire never to reveal her humiliation to anyone, the other was not to let Lord Welham know that his idol had feet of clay. Robin was dead, thankfully, and Lord Welham would never know that his cousin had despised him, not from her lips anyway. How to explain away the missing money was worrying her however.

His lordship had noticed that she had finished eating and was watching her face with interest. He noted her thoughtful look and guessed its cause. When she looked up and saw him regarding her she put her hands up to her hair and pulling it back twisted it tightly together at the back. Since she had lost her pins it would not stay however and began to slowly unwind.

His lordship stood up and came over to her. He removed

the table and said quietly as he sat down, "Are you ready to talk to me now?"

"I do not know what I can say that will be of any use to you."

"Where did you live?", he asked her.

"You know that we were at Cadiz, with Robin in charge of supplies to his battalion. You wrote to him there often."

"Where did you live in Cadiz?" he persisted.

"On the Via Ventura", she replied quickly.

"What number?"

"Sixty-three".

"Think again, Madame", he drawled. "There are no numbers, only names on the Via Ventura."

"Do you know Cadiz then?" she asked warily.

"I visited Robin there and returned to England with him six months before he married you. He was living in barracks then and that was where I wrote to him always."

"I know", she said. Then, "We lived on Esta Rosa."

"With the enlisted men? Why?"

She might have known that he would be informed on everything. She said simply, "Robin said it would be less expensive. He had already mortgaged Cuckfield as far as he could."

"I don't believe you", he said roughly. "I should have known had he done so."

"Oh come, my lord, Robin was twenty-five when he died. He had been in charge of his estate for four years. How could you know whether he had loans on it or not?"

He looked at her for a long time in silence, but since she had told him only the truth she did not flinch from his gaze.

At last he spoke. "Why did you not have any new gowns in all that time?"

"I did not go out so there was no need," she said.

"Did you not attend the battalion dances or visit the other officers' homes then?"

"Robin preferred hunting to dancing," she said desperately, "and mostly in the evenings he went out with his friends."

He looked at her again and said gently, "And what did you do in the evenings, child?"

"I? I kept myself busy. There was a lot to do in the house."

"Such a small house as that kept you busy every evening? How many servants did you have?"

His question took her by surprise as she had been momentarily transported back in time to the squalid little house at Cadiz and so she faltered,

"How many . . . I don't recall." She looked wildly at him and saw his lips tighten. "There was Robin's batman, and . . . and . . ." Her voice died away as he rose from the chair opposite her and came towards her. He reached down into her lap and taking her hands in his turned them over. Even after a year the tell-tale signs were still there. Callouses on her palms, little burns and scars on her fingers. Still holding her hands he asked his question again.

"How many servants did you have?"

"None, oh none, there was not enough money."

"I paid Robin an allowance in addition to his money from his estate. A very handsome allowance, child. More than enough for a house on Via Ventura, several servants and new gowns for you. Yet you lived in squalor on Esta Rosa and did all of the house work too."

"My lord, I have told you more than once that I do not know what Robin did with his money. Maybe he gambled; I don't know. All I do know is that when he died six months after leaving Cadiz, I had to sell his horses and equipment to pay the bills and get enough money to return home. His batman helped me and escorted me to England.

11

When I arrived I was practically penniless and Jim Bates paid my fare on the stage so that I could get to Nanny.'' She pulled her hands away from him and said urgently, ''My goodness . . . Nanny! She will think I am dead. Please will you convey me to the nearest town so that I can get a carriage as quickly as possible.''

His face was implacable as he said, ''Mrs. Rowley you are going nowhere. I would be failing in my duty to my family if I allowed you to set out from my home in the condition that you are in now. In my letter to you, which was in no way dictatorial, I offered you a home here. As the widow of my heir you are entitled to every comfort I have to offer and now that I have found you, here you will remain.'' He turned and picked up her reticule from the small table and shook it as he said with a smile, ''Besides, child, how far do you think you would get with the money you have in here?''

''But Nanny . . . ?'' she whispered imploringly.

''Only furnish me with her whereabouts and a messenger will be sent post-haste to inform her.''

''I am very tired,'' she said tearfully, ''I will consent to remain for tonight only if you will send to Nanny. Her name is Mrs. Manning and she lives outside Cheltenham in a village called Bilbourne.'' She put her hands over her face and wept bitter tears at her own weakness in surrendering.

His lordship rang the bell and, when Porter entered, gave him rapid instructions in an undertone. Whilst she finished weeping and then dried her tears he kept his back turned towards her and she was grateful to him. He came back to her eventually and said, ''How long is it since you have eaten?''

''I had some lunch yesterday,'' she said softly, ''and was hoping to be here and then away in time to stop off at

Jim Bates' house in Cirencester for the night. He had asked me to come over if I needed help,'' she explained.

"However when the wheel came off we were forced to put up for the night at a village inn. I had enough money for a sandwich and coffee that evening and had to pretend I could not eat before travelling in the morning.''

"I cannot understand how it is that you will accept help from Robin's batman and not from me,'' he said.

"But you see, my lord, he gives willingly, not from a sense of duty like you.'' She could have bitten her tongue out the instant she spoke for his lordship's expression became very ugly.

"Thank you for teaching me my manners, Mrs. Rowley,'' he said icily.

"I beg your pardon, my lord,'' she said contritely, "You must forgive me. Sometimes my tongue runs away with me. I was forever in trouble with it at home.''

He raised his eyebrows at her and said still coldly, "But you believe it to be the truth nonetheless.''

She drew a deep breath and then said, "My lord, nothing in the past has induced me to believe that you have anything but contempt for me. Robin let me read your letters in which you refused to come to our wedding, and your own letter to me after Robin's death conveyed only the feeling that it was your duty to care for me. I have no wish to be beholden to someone who considers me beneath him by birth and a burden that he needs must take on.''

Lord Welham, an honest man, was forced to admit to himself that he had considered her an unwelcome burden, but pride would not let him admit it to her. He had discovered, to his surprise, that he was dealing with an adversary with a keen intellect and as any form of learning found favour with him he viewed her with grudging respect.

"You wrong me, Madame,'' he said curtly. "At no time did I ever think that your birth was inferior. Your father was a respectable man, and you know well that your mother's birth could have procured for her any man in the land had she not married your father."

"Was it then my father's chosen profession that made you ask Robin not to marry me?"

"Not so, Madame; I admire any man of learning, as Robin must have told you."

The pink colour that rose to her cheeks puzzled Lord Welham. He was well aware that her father had been a Classics Professor at Oxford and could not think that his knowledge of this could embarrass her in any way.

"Why then?" she asked quickly to hide her feelings. What Robin had said of men of learning and his cousin in particular was her secret.

Still puzzled his lordship replied, "I did not think that Robin was ready to settle down. I was also concerned about a young girl being taken to Spain at that time. You were only sixteen, Mrs. Rowley."

She looked down quickly and did not see his smile. "It is useless to talk, my lord. There is no way that you and I can ever agree I think. My father taught me logic as well as Greek and Latin. My training tells me that you are convinced that you are right and will not be turned. You have an overweening pride in your intellect and will own none your master."

"You accuse me of pride, Mrs. Rowley. Is it not your own pride that will not allow you to accept my hospitality? You resent what you think is careless charity from one who is above you. Since I have never thought myself above you it can only be foolish pride."

She looked up quickly to see a rare and transforming smile on his face and found herself smiling back as she said, "You too have studied logic, my lord."

* * *

Anne Rowley sat up in bed and watched a young chamber-
maid kindling a fire in the grate.

"Oh, Ma'am, I beg your pardon for waking you," the
girl said, "only I dropped the poker."

"It's all right", Anne said kindly, "What time is it?"

"Past eight o'clock, Ma'am," the girl said straightening
up. "Mrs. Porter said I was to leave you 'till the very last,
and on no account was I to wake you." Her expression
became woeful and Anne said quickly, "Never mind, I
won't tell Mrs. Porter if you don't. Is she the housekeeper?

"Yes ma'am, and wife to Mr. Porter, the butler."

"How long has she been housekeeper?"

"Only five years. You see the old Countess wouldn't
'ave an 'ousekeeper, said she liked doing for 'erself. So
when she died five years ago 'is lordship was right cut-up,
them being so close an all, and Porter fetched 'is missus
in temporary until 'is lordship was 'imself again and could
appoint a proper one."

A knock came on the door and the young girl instantly
spun round.

"Come in," Anne called and the door opened to admit
another maid. She was a far superior person to the young
girl and looked to be a few years older than Anne herself.

"Haven't you finished yet, Becky?" she asked severely.

"I am sorry," Anne said, "but I have kept her talking."

"Thank you, ma'am. Excuse me, Liza," the girl muttered as she hurried out. Anne looked enquiringly at Liza
who said, "His lordship has sent me to wait on you, Madame. Would you like your hot chocolate now?"

"Yes please," said Anne, "What time is breakfast usually served?"

"At ten o'clock, Madame. His lordship is an early riser."

Promptly at ten o'clock Anne presented herself in the
small dining-room, having learned its whereabouts from

Liza. Lord Welham was already seated when she entered and she was amused to see the surprise on his face.

"Are you an early riser too, Mrs. Rowley?" he asked.

"Old habits die hard," she answered and seated herself at the other end of the table.

"We cannot possibly converse if you sit down there," he said sharply.

"My Papa detested conversation at breakfast," she replied promptly. "I wonder why I thought you would be the same."

Without replying Lord Welham walked to the sideboard, poured out two cups of coffee and carried them back to his end of the table. He pulled out the chair next to his and looked at her. Since she could think of no good reason for remaining where she was, she capitulated and came to sit beside him. A footman entered carrying several chafing dishes which he set on the sideboard, then commenced to serve them both. She was shocked at the amount of food that was set out for just two people and privately thought it dreadfully wasteful.

"You are not eating much, Mrs. Rowley," said Lord Welham solicitously.

"I do not usually make a large breakfast, my lord. Some bread and butter and coffee is all that I require."

"I think you are a little surprised at the amount of food on my sideboard," he said correctly defining her thoughts.

"Since you mention it first, I am," she answered, "It is very wasteful and I am surprised that your housekeeper has not yet discovered that you dislike fish for breakfast. But perhaps it is her favourite dish and will not be wasted," she finished tartly.

"How do you know that I do not like fish?" he asked.

"The footman did not offer it to you, or to me either, but I know by the smell that it is there."

Lord Welham got up from his seat and crossed to the sideboard. He lifted the cover of the last dish, turned up his nose in distaste and resumed his seat. He smiled at her and asked, "For how long were you your father's house-keeper?"

"From the day my mother died until I married Robin. Two and a half years in all."

"You were very young when you started then, I am surprised your father allowed it."

She smiled to herself rather than him and said fondly, "Papa was only interested in teaching; other things passed him by. Had I not assumed responsibility the house would have ground to a halt. I think he did not notice that I was doing the housekeeping." She drew a sharp breath and added, "It stood me in good stead later." Both then continued to eat in silence.

Lord Welham filled both coffee cups again and then said, "I wish you would tell me what it was like."

She looked up sharply and said, "You have seen the Esta Rosa. Can you not imagine?"

"Yes," he said thoughtfully. "A row of wattle houses with mud floors and a half loft up a ladder. A pump shared by about ten houses and chickens and pigs in the yard. Housekeeping for your father in Oxford could not have prepared you for that."

"I watched the girl kindling the fire in my room this morning and thought how many times I had tried before I got it right. Robin was very angry with me and . . ." She paused.

"And what?" Lord Welham prompted.

"And went to the barracks for breakfast," she finished lamely.

Lord Welham was aware that she had not started to say any such thing. That she was hiding a great deal from him was obvious but he could not, as yet, see any way to make her tell.

"So you did all the cooking and cleaning," he said.

"And the washing and shopping. I became very proficient at haggling in the market in Spanish," she added proudly.

"Who did the heavy work?" his lordship asked lightly. "Bringing in the wood for the fire, carrying the water, turning the mattress?"

She stared at him for a long time in silence. "Sometimes Jim Bates helped," she said stonily. She put down her cup and pushed back her chair said, "When can I return to Cheltenham?"

Lord Welham also pushed back his chair and said firmly, "I sent a letter to Mrs. Manning explaining that you would be staying here indefinitely and asking her if she also would like to come and live here, to be your chaperone."

"How very high-handed of you, Lord Welham, when you knew that I had turned down your offer."

"Out of false pride, Mrs. Rowley. There is no one else to whom you can turn for money or you would not have come to me. Your father's only living relation is an indigent parson, he cannot help you. Your mother's surviving brother is a profligate rake who holds orgies in his mouldering residence and will shortly die penniless and without progeny. You have told me yourself that your nurse cannot support you and yet you wish to return and be a burden to her. I can offer both her and you the comfort, warmth and sustenance that a lady of her years should be entitled to. Would it surprise you to know that she accepted my offer and will be arriving tomorrow."

She jumped up so abruptly that her chair fell to the ground. "You are hateful, Lord Welham, hateful, arrogant and cruel, just like your cousin. How I wish I had never set eyes upon either of you, nor bore the name Rowley.

There is nothing that I can say that will in any way convey just how much I despise you. You work everything round until it suits your own ends, regardless of other people's feelings. Oh how like Robin you are!'' she flung at him with contempt and rushed from the room, leaving a bewildered man to wonder exactly what his cousin could have done to inspire such hatred. That he intended to find out was plain by the look on his face.

When Anne arrived breathless and tearful at her room it was to find it occupied by Liza who was unpacking a small port manteau. The contents were Anne's own and it was plain to her that his lordship had planned well. Liza took one look at her face and said kindly, ''Would you like me to leave, Madame?''

Anne gathered herself together and said calmly, ''No it's all right. I have got myself into a rage and will be better presently.'' She sat down by the window and Liza continued unpacking. After a time she said, ''What is your usual job when I am not here?''

''I'm parlourmaid, Madame, but I have long wanted to be a lady's maid.'' She remained silent so Anne spoke again.

''Why is that?''

''My mother was lady's maid to the Countess until she married. It's a much better position, Madame.''

''And you mother has taught you all she knows I suppose.''

''Yes, Madame.''

''You will not need to know much to tend to the few clothes I have,'' she said with a smile.

''But when the lady from Leamington has been to measure you, Madame, there will be lots for me to do,'' Liza said excitedly.

''What lady from Leamington?'' Anne asked coldly.

Liza was a little frightened, knowing that she had divulged something that his lordship had not yet told Mrs. Rowley. "His lordship has sent for a dressmaker, Madame," she said slowly.

Anne was sorry for the maid and said quietly, "It seems his lordship omitted to inform me of that."

A perfunctory knock on the door heralded the entrance of Lord Welham. He took in the expressions on both girls' faces and decided that Liza had been indiscreet, but said only, "I am sorry I have put you to so much trouble for nothing, Liza, but I have decided that Mrs. Rowley shall have the Blue Suite, she can then enjoy the privacy of her own sitting-room." He turned to Anne and holding out his hand said, "Come with me and I will show it to you." She ignored his hand and sailed out of the room saying, "I have something to say to you, my lord."

The Blue Suite was a delightful apartment comprising a closet and dressing-room, a bedroom and a beautiful L-shaped sitting-room whose longest arm overlooked the front terraces and the main drive. It was situated to the right of the main staircase as you ascended. Lord Welham led Anne into the sitting-room and facing the door she saw three large windows hung with deep blue velvet drapes. It was a beautiful room and Anne's face reflected the beauty she saw.

Lord Welham was well pleased with her reaction and said lightly, "I thought the Green Room would be better suited to Mrs. Manning as it is at the back of the house and will be quieter. I intend to have the communicating room turned into a sitting-room for her."

Anne knew that it behove her to thank Lord Welham for the trouble that he was taking and so she said stiffly, "Thank you very much, Lord Welham. I am sure that Nanny will be very comfortable."

"Are you indeed resigned to your fate, Mrs. Rowley? If you are, will you let me tell you that I have meant it all for the best. You were a pitiful sight when you arrived yesterday and though I admit that my first invitation was delivered from a sense of duty, my subsequent actions have been governed by a desire to eradicate the privations that I know you must have suffered in Spain." His lordship spoke sincerely but his unfortunate reference to Spain fanned the spark of anger in Anne.

"Did you also think that ordering a dressmaker from Leamington without asking me would make me happy?" she asked angrily.

Lord Welham laughed and said, "There you have me I'm afraid. I had meant to inform you this morning, but you left the breakfast table somewhat precipitately."

"To inform me, not ask me," she said scathingly.

"Well as to that," he returned lightly, "if you think I am going to ask my friends for dinner and have you sit down in a three-year-old gown you must think again. You may not care what my friends think of me but I do, and I have my reputation as a leader of fashion to think of."

She looked at him with scorn and said, "I have no need to dine with you when your friends are here."

"No need, no," he said, "but I thought you would like to meet some young men and women of your own class again. You are very young and will probably be thinking of marriage later on."

"You are wrong, my lord, I want no more of marriage. Once was enough." She turned her back on him and went to the window and after a moment heard the door bang behind him.

Liza entered tentatively from the bedroom and said, "Would you like to change to another dress, Madame?"

Anne was aware suddenly how creased her dress was and realised with a shock that she had worn it for three whole days. "Yes please", she said, "Though what to change it for I don't know."

''There is that nice green cotton one with long sleeves,'' Liza said instantly. ''It's still quite warm although it is October.''

Dressed in the green-striped dress decorated with green ribbons Anne began to feel a little calmer, but when Liza suggested brushing out her hair and dressing it a bit more fancy Anne replied repressingly. ''I like it as it is thank you.'' Liza was sorry because she privately thought that with a few curls about her face and an odd ringlet over one shoulder Mrs. Rowley could look quite pretty.

When the dressmaker came down the main staircase later on that day, Porter was waiting in the hall to convey her to the library.

''Ah, Mrs. Wilbraham,'' his lordship said, ''please come in and sit down.'' Mrs. Wilbraham was not used to dealing with fine gentlemen so she sat gingerly on the edge of the seat. ''You have taken Mrs. Rowley's measurements I believe and shown her your pattern cards.''

''Yes, my lord,'' she answered.

''You understand that I wish Mrs. Rowley to be dressed in the height of fashion?'' She nodded.

''What I require, Mrs. Wilbraham, is half a dozen morning and afternoon gowns, three or four evening gowns and two ball gowns.''

Mrs. Wilbraham was startled and delighted at the size of the order and said, ''Everything will be of the best, my lord.''

''Of course,'' he replied. ''Undergarments, nightdresses and wraps will be required as well, and any other adjuncts that you feel necessary,'' he added.

''Stockings and shoes,'' she supplied excitedly.

''Everything,'' he stated firmly, ''And I would like them delivered as they become ready. You have seen the young lady's colouring and can choose the right colours I am sure.'' Mrs. Wilbraham nodded again. ''But what I want immediately is a riding-habit.''

Anne came slowly down the main staircase and stood irresolutely in the hall. She had come to make her peace with Lord Welham much against her instincts. With the arrival of Nanny on the following day her fate would be sealed. Mrs. Wilbraham's arrival had made her realise what no words of his lordship had been able to. She was destitute and alone in a world that had nothing to offer to a lonely, poor, young gentlewoman. There was nowhere that she could turn but to Lord Welham, and although she disliked him intensely she must live with him, at least for the present. She had thought of asking Mrs. Wilbraham if she could work for her but the feeling of humiliation that had assailed her at the thought had finally made up her mind. She had a proposition to put to his lordship and if he was agreeable would go some way towards assuaging her feelings at his victory. She turned to find Porter beside her and enquired if his lordship was in the library. On learning that he was she crossed the hall and knocked on the door. When she entered Lord Welham was seated at his ease, in a wing-chair by the fire reading a book. He rose instantly and led her to the opposite chair then leant on the mantlepiece.

He looked at her enquiringly and she said softly, ''It seems that you have won, my lord, and I *must* remain here. That being so I would like to do something with my time to repay you for your kindness.''

''I wish for no repayment, Mrs. Rowley,'' he said kindly, ''It seems that my family should repay you for what you have suffered at our hands.''

She looked at him sharply, then down again quickly and said, ''It is not so, my lord, but I do not wish to speak of it. I have noticed that your housekeeper seems unable to do the amount of work that must fall on her. Therefore I would like to help in that way.''

23

"Certainly not," he said sharply. "I did not invite you to stay in order that you should do the work I pay my servants for."

"But I should enjoy it," she said gently. "I am not used to being idle. Why even at Nanny's I arranged the flowers and washed the ornaments. Your pewter is sadly neglected and it's high time the rugs in the hall were washed before the really bad weather comes. Please will you not let me organise such things for you?"

"I have servants and a housekeeper to do those jobs," he said.

"But, you stupid man," she said exasperated, "they are not being done. Your housekeeper is worse than useless. If you will not let me do it then I warn you, my lord, at the first opportunity, I shall leave this place. I will not live on charity." She rose as she spoke and made for the door, then turned in the centre of the room as if afraid. She was surprised to see his lordship still where she had left him with a wide grin on his face.

"The last person who called me stupid was lying on the floor a moment later. From whom did you inherit your dreadful temper, child?"

She smiled back and said, "Did I truly call you stupid, my lord. If so I beg your pardon, but I did warn you of my wayward tongue."

"I accept your apology, Mrs. Rowley," he said bowing mockingly, "but let *me* warn you that any attempt to leave my protection will go ill with you."

"Then I can help the housekeeper," she persisted.

"Do as you wish," he said in a bored voice and turned to his chair.

The next morning Anne dressed quickly and was downstairs a half-hour before breakfast. As she suspected she was in time to apprehend Mrs. Porter as she left the small dining-room.

"Good morning, Madame," Mrs. Porter said respectfully.

"Good morning," Anne replied. "You are Mrs. Porter, the housekeeper I believe."

Mrs. Porter replied stiffly. "That's right, Madame."

"Just the person I wanted to see," Anne said, mixing with dexterous skill the right amount of deference and authority in her voice. His lordship proceeding down the long corridor from the stable door, halted in his tracks and unashamedly listened to the ensuing conversation.

"I have not had the opportunity until now for thanking you for the excellent arrangements you have made both for myself and Mrs. Manning. My own rooms are delightful and a credit to your skill. However do you manage to run this entire household unaided?" His lordship would have applauded had he been able. Mrs. Porter however was completely won over and replied, "It isn't easy, Madame, not with the sort of girl we get nowadays."

"I'm sure it isn't," Anne replied instantly. "I was used to running my father's establishment before I married and although it could not compare in size to Welham Abbey, it was the little jobs that I found the most tiresome. You know, washing the ornaments, arranging flowers, writing out the menus. There never seemed enough time in one day for them all."

"How right you are, Madame," Mrs. Porter said, warming to the theme. "Many's the night I have sat up till all hours writing the menus for the next day."

Anne paused as if struck by a sudden thought. "Mrs. Porter," she said excitedly, "Why don't I help you out? Here I am with nothing in the world to do to occupy my time, and there you are rushed off your feet. Will you let me try my hand at the menus and the flowers, then if you

25

think of any other little thing I could do later, I would willingly take it on."

"Well, I don't know as how his lordship would like it," she mused.

"Leave his lordship to me," Anne said briskly, "and if you wouldn't mind, Mrs. Porter, perhaps you would inform the cook before I see him today. Shall we say at eleven o'clock in the servants' hall." Thus vanquished and dismissed Mrs. Porter made her bewildered way through the door to the servants' quarters.

Lord Welham emerged from the corridor and said, "Hooked, played and landed, Mrs. Rowley. Accept my compliments on a masterly performance."

"Were you listening?" Anne said severely.

"I wouldn't have missed it for the world," his lordship said, "particularly the bit about me."

After visiting the cook and getting the menus for the next day, Anne retired to her sitting-room to sit in the window and watch the drive for the first sign of a carriage. His lordship had told her at breakfast that he had sent his own carriage and the second groom to fetch Mrs. Manning the day before.

At last, just before luncheon was habitually served, in the small dining-room, she saw a carriage coming up the drive. Repressing her first instinct, which was to rush down the stairs, she waited until the carriage stopped before proceeding gracefully down to the hall. She could not, however, stop herself from rushing into the arms of the small spry lady who stepped into the hall.

"Now, now, Miss Anne dear, don't get yourself into such a taking. Here I am large as life, and glad to be here. Now do calm down and let me greet his lordship, who is waiting, or he will think I have lost my manners."

After luncheon Anne and Mrs. Manning went upstairs

to see that lady's apartments. "My this is fine, this is very fine," said Mrs. Manning looking around her. "What a dear kind man Lord Welham is to be sure. Going to all this trouble just for me."

"I don't find him all that kind," Anne said petulantly, "You have done nothing but sing his praises since you arrived. He is arrogant, overbearing and selfish."

"And you are thankless, graceless and bad mannered," said Mrs. Manning tartly, "What has the man done except offer you a home, clothes and a chaperone, I would like to know?"

"Oh Nanny, you don't know him. He has appeared all chivalry to you no doubt, but he has forced me to stay and dragged you here willy-nilly without once asking if it is what we want."

"Men are often like that," said Mrs. Manning placatingly, "They don't mean to be arrogant, it's just that they are used to having things all their own way. They foolishly think that we need looking after all the time. Not that you don't need looking after, my girl," she said to Anne's look of scorn, "And *I* had no notion which way to turn. If you ask me Lord Welham is a blessing in disguise and I for one am glad to be in this nice warm house now that winter is coming."

"But Nanny I had my own plans, the milliner's shop, and he wouldn't listen to me."

"No more did I think he would, when you set out on that venture. Stands to reason a fine gentleman like he is won't want someone in his family setting up in trade, and there's no use you glaring at me like that, Miss Anne, because your own Mama and Papa would have turned their noses up at it as well."

Anne knew herself beaten. Nanny had her exactly where she wanted her and she had no argument, because her nurse had warned her not to marry Robin in the first place.

TWO

"*Well, what is it this time?*" *Anne said to herself as* she climbed the stairs to her sitting-room carrying a large dressmaker's box. The morning and afternoon dresses she had already received together with quantities of fine lawn undergarments and night-wear seemed to her quite sufficient for her needs. She had however been pleased with the pale green silk evening gown with silk stockings and fine kid sandals, for to tell the truth she *had* felt dowdy especially after Lord Welham's two houseguests had arrived the week before.

After going along tolerably well for three or four weeks Lord Welham had announced that he had two friends arriving who would be staying with him until after Christmas. Anne, in her new role as assistant housekeeper, had taken great pains to bring the house into order and had received praise from Lord Welham for her efforts. This had secretly gratified her and so they had been in charity with each other much to Mrs. Manning's delight. The two guests had surprised her for she had expected to meet, what she called, his lordship's arrogance in any friend of his.

Lord Stone proved to be tall, good-looking and softly spoken, with a gentle manner and a lively intellect. He was a Baron and lived with his widowed mother fifty miles away. He laughingly admitted to Anne that he was relieved to be away from her for a while as she was an anxious worrying sort of person. Before the week was out he was calling her Anne and she calling him Ivor. Lord Accres, a Viscount, was also pleased to leave his doting parents. As he was their only child they were anxious to see him married and kept inviting hopeful young ladies for his inspection. Lord Accres however had a problem, he was incurably shy with young ladies and though just as intelligent as his two friends, invariably appeared stupid and gauche when ladies were present. Anne set him at his ease instantly by ignoring his stutters and mistakes and talking to him about 'Euclid'. So he became Freddy and she Anne and a grateful Lord Accres confided to his friends that she was the only young lady he could talk to.

*Reaching her sitting-room Anne opened the box and dis-*covered to her horror an elegant riding-habit in dark green velvet. She sat down on her sofa and contemplated it with misery. Only Nanny knew of her abiding fear of horses and she had no wish to tell the hard riding Lord Welham of it, since she considered it a weakness.

"Why didn't the stupid man ask me first," she said angrily, "I could have told him then that I do not ride." She rose quickly and went to find Nanny.

"He has bought me a riding-habit, Nanny. What shall I do?"

"Why tell him of course," Nanny replied promptly.

"Never," Anne said instantly, "Tell him I am afraid of horses and have him revile me for it. Not I."

"Overweening pride," Nanny answered, "and why should he revile you? You are not the first young lady to be afraid of horses, nor won't be the last."

"He has bought the habit; he won't be pleased that I can't use it," said Anne trying to justify her stand.

"Nonsense, you have only to tell him and all will be well."

Seeing no help forthcoming from her nurse, Anne went in search of Lord Welham. Her anger at her own fear became anger at him, for putting her in this awkward position, so that when she found him alone in his gun room she said sharply,

"Had you asked me first before ordering a riding-habit for me, I could have informed you that I do not ride."

"Then I will teach you," he answered without looking up from the cleaning of his gun.

Anne stamped her foot angrily. "I do not ride, I do not wish to ride, and I will not be taught by you," she stated.

Lord Welham looked up and seeing her flashing eyes jumped to the wrong conclusion.

"What an ungrateful child you are," he said flatly, "Did your Mother never teach you to accept gifts graciously?"

"I am not a child and I told you right at the beginning I wanted nothing from you. You think to ride rough-shod over me, Lord Welham, and win my approval with unsolicited gifts. You are far out if you think I am so easily won."

Lord Welham's fragile temper snapped also. "If this is the way you treated Robin I am not surprised that he housed you in the Esta Rosa. It was probably to keep you away from the censure of his fellow officers."

Anne took one step back and then stood as if turned to stone.

Lord Welham continued, too angry now to be sorry, "You will ride Madame, you will ride tomorrow morning at seven. My friends and I will be waiting for you. Do not delay us."

He put down his gun and marched from the room, slamming the door behind him. Anne sank down into a chair and burst into surprised tears.

*At dinner that evening Mrs. Manning tried to keep the con-*versation going. It was not easy, as Lord Welham and Anne, whenever their eyes met, glared at each other balefully and the two guests, sensing the atmosphere, were at a loss to know what to do. Mrs. Manning retired early to bed and Anne, after talking half-heartedly to Ivor and Freddy, decided to retire also. Lord Welham went to open the drawing-room door for her and as she passed she looked up at him. The approaching morning and the terror it held prompted her to tell him of her fear.

"Lord Welham will you please listen to . . ." She got no further. "Tomorrow at seven," he said firmly, and closed the door behind her.

*Liza roused Anne at half an hour after six the next morn-*ing. "Come along, Madame," she said, "His lordship told me to have you ready by seven o'clock."

"I am not going," Anne said desperately, "I cannot go." She put her hands over her face and Liza, a kindly young woman, said, "I think his lordship will be angry if you do not."

"Liza, I am afraid to ride," Anne said through her hands.

"Does his lordship know?" Liza asked surprised.

"I tried to tell him last night, he would not listen." Anne took her hands down. "Help me, Liza. I am afraid," she said.

Her face was indeed very pale and Liza sat beside her and put an arm around her. "His lordship is not cruel my dear," she said. "Only tell him this morning and he will understand."

"He doesn't care," Anne wailed. "Stay with me, Liza, help me to tell him." Liza reassured her and helped her into a wrap. She wandered aimlessly from one room to the other looking at the ormolu clock on the mantlepiece in the sitting-room. Seven o'clock came and went and Anne got more agitated.

"Perhaps they will ride off when I don't come," she said, "Do you think so, Liza?"

Her question was answered at ten minutes after seven, when her sitting-room door burst open and Lord Welham stormed in. He looked angrily at both young girls and turned to Liza said, "Out." Liza fled to the bedroom.

Anne tried to speak but Lord Welham in a towering rage was unstoppable.

"You will put your habit on in five minutes and come downstairs," he raged, "I have waited long enough for your childish behaviour to abate. Now go!"

Speech deserted Anne as fear of Lord Welham, in a rage such as she had never seen before, seized her.

"I . . . I . . . can . . . afraid . . ." she stammered.

He towered over her, and grasping her shoulders shook her. "*GO AND GET CHANGED*," he shouted.

She uttered a strangled, "No, I can't."

Grasping her wrap he pulled it down over her shoulders, and beside himself with rage he hissed, "If you do not go now I will strip you and put you into the habit myself." He saw her terror but could no longer control himself.

Anne tore herself from his grasp and gasped. "I will go, . . . I will go . . . please don't touch me."

She fled to the bedroom and closed the door. Liza helped her trembling mistress into the habit and full of misery herself for the poor girl said softly, "When his rage goes, my dear, he will be sorry. His mother used to say he would hang for his temper one day, but he is always very sorry afterwards."

Anne's face was pale as wax when she came from the bedroom, and no expression of any kind registered on her features as she walked towards Lord Welham. What he, in his temper, took to be sullen defiance was really frozen terror. He took her arm and led her from the house, towards the stables and through the archway into the stable-yard. Lord Stone, seated astride a large chestnut mare, was at the other side of the yard. Of Lord Accres there was no sign.

"Freddy has gone for a canter; his horse was getting restless," he called out.

Lord Welham led Anne to a mounting-block and forced her to climb it. Standing at one side was a quiet-looking brown horse with a groom at its head. Nearby a fierce-looking black stallion was snorting and twitching his ears. Anne heard Lord Welham speaking to her but was not sure what he said. He spoke again and she tried to listen, " . . . then swing your leg over the pommel." He pushed her round and she found herself sitting on the saddle. She obediently swung her leg over and he fitted her feet in the stirrups. Reins were thrust into her numb hands and at that moment Lord Stone rode over. He looked at her face and saw the blank look in her eyes.

"I say Oliver, I don't think you should you know," he said concernedly. "The poor girl is terrified."

"Foolish pride and temper," Lord Welham said without looking at her and strode away to mount his horse. Now that he had her in the saddle his temper had almost disappeared and he rode over to take the leading-rein with a smile on his lips. Ivor noted the way that Anne flinched as the big horse came near her and carefully kept out of her vision. With Lord Welham leading they walked out of the stable-yard and into the park, towards a gate in a fence. As they approached the gate Freddy came thundering across the grass and pulled his horse round to follow them. Unfortunately for Anne his horse collided with the back of hers and that docile creature leapt with fear. The leading-rein was snatched from Lord Welham's hand and lacking guidance from his rider the horse galloped towards the fence and jumped. Anne, unseated by the jump, fell to the ground with a sickening thud and screamed. All three men galloped towards her and struggling to sit up she cried out, "No! No!"

Ivor immediately dismounted and shouted to his friends, "Keep your horses back, she's afraid of them."

In that moment Lord Welham grasped the enormity of what he had done to her and leaping from his saddle, thrust the reigns into Ivor's hand. He ran to where Anne was lying and as he lifted her into his arms she cried out with pain and cradled her left arm with her right, "I think it is broken, my lord," she gasped. He looked down at her lying in his arms. He saw her pale face, he felt her trembling body and with deep compassion he said, "Please try to forgive me, child, for I am truly sorry for what I have done to you this day."

Anne looked up at him and in a pain-filled voice said, "I think I am going to swoon again."

Lying her gently on her bed he said to Liza, "Pull her boots off then go to my room and fetch my razor." When Liza returned he had removed the skirt of her habit and her petticoat.

"My lord," she said outraged, "I will undress her if you will go away."

"Don't be a fool, Liza, you will never cut this jacket off alone. She has broken her arm."

"But, my lord," she persisted.

"Come on, Liza, before she comes round," he said roughly, "She is nothing but a child." Liza privately thought that his lordship might have a shock when he removed the jacket, for she knew full well that Mrs. Rowley had a woman's body beneath her clothes.

Lord Welham skillfully slit the sleeve of the jacket and with Liza's help removed it. Anne shifted slightly and moaned then lay still on the bed, clad only in her chemise and stockings. Lord Welham looked at her for a moment only, then turned away and walked to the fire. Liza hastily covered her mistress with the bedclothes and slightly flushed said, "Will the doctor be long, my lord?"

Lord Welham turned and said, "Lord Accres went for him immediately; he should be here shortly." He walked over to the bed and said softly, "Why didn't you tell me child that you were afraid?"

Liza, greatly bold, said defensively, "She tried last night, my lord, but you would not listen."

He swung round to look at her, then turning back to regard Anne he said, "I was in a rage. Curse my temper, it turned me into a fool."

Anne stirred again then spoke softly, "My arm hurts, how it hurts, my head too." She opened her eyes suddenly then grimaced with pain. "My lord," she said surprised.

"Lie still," he said softly. "The doctor will be here presently." He sat on the bed beside her and carefully removing the pins from her hair, felt her head gently until her grimace of pain helped him to locate the lump.

"The skin is not broken," he said, "but you have a large lump."

She lay very still with her lips gripped tightly together so that he knew she was in great pain.

"What a strange mixture of courage and fear you are, child." He stroked the hair back from her forehead and felt the fine dew of sweat that had broken out on her.

The door opened to admit Mrs. Manning. "My little lamb," she said gently, "what have you done to yourself?"

"It is I who have done it, Mrs. Manning," Lord Welham said contritely. "*My* foolish pride and temper, and I am sincerely sorry for it."

He put his hand over his eyes for a moment and Anne,

surprised at his humility, found herself saying, "No, my lord, my foolish pride in not telling you." Only then did tears start from her eyes and Mrs. Manning bustled Lord Welham out saying, "Leave her with me, my lord, for the moment."

"You will need me when the doctor comes," he said grimly.

"I know and I will call you then," she said.

The doctor's examination caused Anne great discomfort and when, with Lord Welham and Mrs. Manning's help, he set her arm, she swooned away again from the intense pain.

Leaving Anne to the care of Mrs. Manning and Liza, Lord Welham went in search of his friends and found them in the withdrawing-room on the first floor. One look at their faces told him all he needed to know. Freddy was blaming himself for the accident and Ivor was blaming his lordship.

"The arm is set," he said grimly, "She showed great courage and fortitude but the pain caused her to pass out again. The doctor says three days in bed because of the blow on her head, and a month before he removes the splint."

"Oh, God," Freddy moaned and put his head in his hands.

"Come, Freddy," Lord Welham said kindly, "How can you blame yourself when it is obvious that I am the one at fault."

"You own it then," Lord Stone said calmly.

"Did you think I would not, Ivor?" said his friend sharply.

"Now that you have come down out of the boughs I did expect it," Ivor said with a smile.

"But it was me, my stupidity as always," said Freddy.

"No, Freddy. My stupidity and my cursed temper," his

lordship replied, "Ivor saw it and I would not listen to him."

"It's true, Freddy," Ivor said gently. "Oliver knows it, and so do I."

A knock at the door interrupted their conversation and Mrs. Manning entered. To everyone's considerable surprise she went to Freddy and said, "Lord Accres, would you come to Mrs. Rowley's room? She will not take her laudanum until she has seen you."

"Mrs. Manning?" his lordship said anxiously.

"It's all right, my lord," she answered, "She says she wants to set his mind at rest before she goes to sleep."

When Freddy had gone with Mrs. Manning, Ivor turned to his friend and said, "Why do you and she fight so much, Oliver?"

"I don't know," Oliver said thoughtfully, "Everything I do for her seems to anger her more. If she had only said I don't ride because I am afraid of horses all would have been well. Instead she shouted at me for ordering a habit for her without asking her first."

"Would you have done that, Oliver?"

"Done what?"

"Admitted a weakness to anyone."

"But this was not a weakness," he said puzzled.

"It was to her," Ivor replied. "How much like you she is. You should understand her better than anyone."

"What is that supposed to mean?" said Oliver coldly.

"That you are both fiery, independent and proud. I wonder how you would have reacted to someone ordering your life in the way that you have ordered hers." He smiled as he spoke to show there was no malice in his words, but Oliver frowned and shook his head. "Well, if you looked at her like that when she first arrived I don't wonder that she is afraid of you."

Oliver's head jerked round and he said in fury, "She is not afraid of me."

"Then why did she come meekly with you, looking like a frozen statue instead of fighting all the way. She really is terrified of horses you know."

"She came because I . . . ," he stopped and thought back. "I thought because I threatened to dress her myself, but now that I think of it, when I took hold of her it was not modesty but terror I saw on her face, as if she thought I would hit her. That first day when she came here I caught hold of her shoulders and I saw the same look then, before she swooned. Why should she think that I would hurt her, Ivor?"

Ivor stood very still with no expression on his face and looked at his friend.

"Why, Ivor? What do you know that I do not?"

"Nothing, how should I?" But Ivor's face now showed concern. "I had never met her until I came here and you introduced her as Robin's widow."

"Robin!" said Oliver with conviction. "You know something of Robin."

Ivor shook his head. "Come, Ivor, I am not a fool. What have you heard that I have not?"

"Nothing that I can tell *you*, Oliver, so do not ask me. You loved the boy, he is dead, there is nothing to say." But Oliver saw the look of revulsion on Ivor's face.

"Nothing to say because I loved him. What did I love then? A monster? Damn you, Ivor, tell me!"

Ivor looked long at his friend before he spoke. "Always remember, Oliver, that I did not want to tell you. Neither does she if what you have told me is true. Everyone knows and always has known that you loved him. He told people you know, that you would give him anything he wanted, because you loved him."

"Get on with it, Ivor," Lord Welham said harshly.

"You remember the summer term when we were fifteen? You invited me home with you for the holidays. When we arrived we were in the middle of a tragedy. Your mother's old dresser, Mrs. Draper, wasn't it? Her son had drowned in the lake and Robin had seen it. Your mother said he was dreadfully upset and you went to comfort him. Do you remember?"

"Yes, I remember," Lord Welham said puzzled, "What of it?"

"Your father's gamekeeper had dived in to try to save the boy and all the servants were talking about it. I went down to the stables where the gamekeeper was drying out and I heard him talking. He said that Robin stood on the bank and smiled all the time. What he couldn't understand was why Robin did not try to save the boy. He was a strong swimmer, you taught him yourself. I heard later that Liza Draper, the boy's older sister, had been there also and she said that Robin pushed her brother out of the boat, then rowed to the shore and watched him drown."

"But he was terribly upset for days after," Oliver protested, "He wouldn't leave the house for a week."

"These are things I heard, Oliver, I don't *know*. It took a year for the story to reach my parents' home. You know the way these things travel. You would know however if it is true that Mrs. Draper is paid an annuity for life, that would have been in your father's will."

"Are you suggesting that my parents knew and kept quiet about it?" Oliver asked coldly.

"The story goes that after the funeral your father was told, but that Mrs. Draper, knowing how much your mother loved Robin, insisted that her old mistress be kept in ignorance. The girl was sworn to secrecy by her mother and from that day on was not allowed to play with Robin."

"My father knew and did nothing? I don't believe it."

"Oh come, Oliver, you know how stiff-necked your

father was. The boy was dead. On the word of a village child would he be likely to drag the name of Rowley through the courts. Luckily for him, your mother's dresser retained her affection for her mistress and happily had obedient children. Liza works here, doesn't she? Ask her and see if she will tell, now your mother has gone.''

Lord Welham turned away and walked the length of the room and back before speaking,

"You have accused my cousin of murder. Is there anything else?'' he asked bitterly.

"I have accused him of nothing. I have only told you what I heard. Remember I did not want to tell you, Oliver, but you insisted.

"Is there anything else?'' Lord Welham spoke with controlled anger and Lord Stone rose from his seat and walked to the door.

"I will pack my bags and leave,'' he said quietly, "I have no desire to see you in yet another raging passion today, since the first one was so disastrous.'' He turned to open the door.

"Ah, God, Ivor,'' his friend said with a moan, "Please forgive me. It is so hard to take it in,'' he put his head in his hands and spoke again, "Come back, Ivor, I must hear it all now.''

Lord Stone came back and sat facing his friend, "There are so many other stories, Oliver. A young doxy in town who was beaten nearly to death, small boys when he was at school, even horses and dogs. Whether they are true or not I have no way of knowing.''

"All hurt, by Robin, and no one told me?''

"Why should they? You wouldn't have believed them. You doted on that boy from the moment he came to live here. I tried to tell you once about a puppy, before the drowning, you shouted me down, so I didn't try again, and your temper is well known to everyone.''

"Am I blind, stupid and ignorant? What am I that I couldn't see? I even let him marry that poor child. What did he do to her, Ivor?"

"Well, you did try to stop it," said his friend placatingly.

"Halfheartedly. He wanted it so much you see. But why should he hurt her? He loved her."

"Did he, Oliver? I have no evidence that he loved anyone but himself. As to why he married her I don't know, but that he had a reason is without doubt. On reaching Cadiz he took her straight to the Esta Rosa. Why?"

"She says because he had no money. She is right when she says he mortgaged Cuckfield before their marriage. I have seen the papers, but what happened to the allowance that I sent him, and her portion? I don't know anything and she won't tell me."

"Would you tell if you had been ill-treated and humiliated. I doubt it, I know I wouldn't."

"She told me once, when she was very angry, that I was cruel, just like my cousin. Do you think that is why she was afraid of me?"

"Possibly. She lived with him for almost two years, and I think if she was not so courageous she might well have died. From the stories I have heard, mental as well as physical cruelty were the weapons he used against those weaker than himself."

Both men relapsed into silence and only the logs crackling in the hearth punctuated their thoughts. Freddy, greatly restored by his conversation with Anne, was puzzled by their woeful expressions and said brightly, "I say you two, what's put you in the dumps? She really is a remarkable woman you know, Oliver, and I feel much better after talking to her."

The glum faces that they turned to him mystified him

and Oliver's remark did not in any way help. "Does *he* know?" he said to Ivor.

"Yes, he knows," Ivor replied.

After dinner Lord Welham insisted that Mrs. Manning should stay with his friends in the drawing-room whilst he went to sit with the invalid. He sent Liza packing also and told her that if she wished to sit up all night with her mistress then she must get some rest.

"How are you feeling now?" he asked gently.

"My head feels a lot better," Anne said resolutely. "But your arm still pains you?"

"Well yes, but I expected it to you know. When Mrs. Thomas' little boy broke his arm he screamed all night for they did not have enough money for laudanum. I was grateful for that at least because mine is not as painful as it was at first. I have been asleep for nine hours you know."

"I know," he said smiling, "Who was Mrs. Thomas?"

"She was Sergeant Thomas' wife and lived next door to me in Esta Rosa. She was a very kind lady and showed me how to do many things that I had no knowledge of." She frowned and then continued, "Did you know that if your chicken is very old, and hard to pluck, you have only to put it in boiling water for a moment and then it is easily done."

"No, I didn't know that," he said gravely, "She must have been a great comfort to you."

"Well, she was, except Robin got angry if he knew I had been speaking to her, so I had to be very careful." She looked at him suddenly and said in a small voice, "I don't wish to talk about Spain any more."

"Then let's talk about something else," he said lightly. "Perhaps you will be angry with me but I would like to give you a present when you are well again. It's my way of saying I am sorry, which I know you don't want to hear.''

''You have no reason to be sorry,'' Anne said stiffly.

''That's easy enough to say, but if I still feel guilty even after you tell me I am not to blame, what other way can I salve my conscience except by giving you a gift.''

''I had forgotten you studied logic,'' she said with a smile.

He smiled back and said, ''If I tell you what I think would be a good gift, will you tell me truthfully if you would like it?'' She nodded.

''A pony and trap?''

''I don't drive either you see,'' she said apologetically.

''But if you would like it, one of the young grooms could drive you.''

She gave him a radiant smile, ''Thank you, my lord, that would be a very useful present.''

''It will be here as soon as you are able to go out,'' he announced. He looked at her hair spread out around her on the pillow in soft curls and said curiously, ''Will you tell me something that has puzzled me from the first moment that I saw you. You have such beautiful hair and yet you scrape it back unbecomingly. Why?'' He was immediately aware that his question had upset her, as that withdrawn look that he knew so well, came over her face. He continued however, gently, ''Was it something that Robin said to you, I wonder?''

Her eyes opened wide and she said involuntarily, ''How did you know?''

''I guessed.''

A faraway look came into her eyes and she said defensively, ''I used to think that my hair was beautiful even if I was not, but Robin said it was too red and made people stare at me. He made me take it all back, he said curls were out of fashion. I did it to please him.'' A small tear gathered in the corner of one eye and ran down her cheek. "Do you truly think it beautiful or is it just because you think you have hurt me that you say so?"

Lord Welham swallowed a lump in his throat and managed to say calmly, "I think it is very beautiful because it is, and for that reason only." He was glad that Anne was not looking at him for he had just made a startling discovery. Looking at that tear running down her cheek he had had a burning desire to take her in his arms and kiss her. He had been in love twice when very young, and both affairs had ended disastrously. After that he had confined himself to obliging ladies on the fringes of society, thinking that when he married it would be to some well brought up young lady, high on the social ladder, who would understand what was expected of a countess. Had anyone told him that he would fall hopelessly in love with a slip of a girl, fifteen years his junior and with no claim to beauty, he would have snubbed them severely. But here he was at five and thirty, mesmerised by one little tear falling down the pale, pain-drawn cheek of the most irritating, argumentative child it had ever been his misfortune to meet.

She brushed the tear away impatiently and said in a whisper, "How soon will it be before I can have some more laudanum please?"

Lord Welham sat with her until Liza returned at eleven by which time Anne was soundly asleep again. He had spent the time whilst she slept thinking about his cousin. He understood now what Ivor had meant by mental cruelty. To make a young girl despise that one thing that gave her confidence in herself was cruel indeed. That it had been done in such a calculating way was something that, as yet, he could not link to the charming boy he had thought he knew through and through.

THREE

Two days later Anne sat up in bed and announced, "I am getting up this morning."

"But, Madame," Liza said instantly, "The doctor said three days."

"Well it is three days if you count the day of my accident. I am going to go into my sitting-room and lie on the sofa, as I am tired of looking at the same wall all day." So saying she swung her legs out of bed and stood up. A wave of dizziness came over her and she sat down on the edge of the bed. Liza came to her immediately, "Get back into bed please, Madame, his lordship will be very angry if you get up."

This was all Anne needed. "Liza," she said firmly, "I am going to the sofa in the other room with or without your help. You may bring a rug to cover me."

Liza ran forward to help her, "Let me put your wrap on first, Madame."

With Liza's help she was laid gently on a bank of cushions at one end of the sofa and a rug was put over her. She had just finished her breakfast when Lord Welham came through from her bedroom.

"What are you doing in here?" he demanded, "You

were not to get up until tomorrow, why didn't you stop her, Liza?''

"She couldn't," Anne announced.

"Well, I can," he replied promptly, and taking the rug from her, he picked her up in his arms and carried her towards the bedroom door.

"Oh please," she said imploringly, "I was so bored in there and if I am lying down does it matter so much in which room I am?" He stopped and looked down at her and to Liza's surprise, smiled softly and said, "I suppose not. Very well young lady you win, but if you put one foot off that sofa Liza is to ring the bell." He put her gently down on the sofa and put the rug over her. He looked down at her startled face and said, "Francis the footman will answer the bell and *he* will be under orders from me to carry you back to bed instantly."

She smiled up at him, "Very well, my lord, I will be good, and thank you."

"You had better be," he said good-naturedly. "I am going out this morning and will be taking Mrs. Manning with me. She has become rather tired from looking after you. As I am visiting the Home Farm on business I have decided to drive over and take her with me for an airing."

"Yes, she is looking rather pulled," Anne said anxiously. "She is very old, you know, but will not admit it. How kind of you to think of her."

Lord Welham departed and Liza watched him go interestedly. From the moment he had looked down at Anne in his arms, and smiled, Liza had studied him carefully. "If he isn't in love," she thought, "I don't know one from two." The situation intrigued her because she was almost sure that her mistress had no idea that Lord Welham loved her. Liza had grown very fond of Anne who was a kind girl and very undemanding of her maid. That young lady was pretty sure that Anne had spent a very unpleasant two years married to Robin, for she could tell things about him that even Lord Stone did not know. She made up her mind that Lord Welham, who she knew to be a kind man at heart, in spite of his temper, would make Anne Rowley an excellent husband. But how to make Anne believe that was something that taxed Liza's brain.

*Youth, resilience, good food and care soon had Anne re-*stored to health, so that when the splint finally came off she was stronger than she had been for three years. Liza was happily employed in letting out the seams of her new dresses, roses appeared in her cheeks for the first time and with her hair carefully dressed by Liza, Mrs. Manning was prompted to tell his lordship that now he saw her as she had been before. "She was never beautiful like her Mama, whom I also nursed from a baby, but with her pretty hair and sparkling eyes we were always well pleased with her appearance."

His lordship agreed, but could not get from his mind the pathetic waif that he had taken in nearly two months ago. This pretty child might well have appealed to Robin.

A few days after the removal of the splint Lord Welham sent a message to Anne asking if she would come to see him in the library. He was sitting on the edge of his desk when she came in and he smiled warmly at her. When she was seated he said, "I have asked you here because I need some help with certain plans I have made for Christmas."

"My help?" she asked intrigued.

"Yes, why not? You have been advising Mrs. Porter ever since you came here. How could I leave you out of my plans? Will you help me?"

"What shall I have to do?"

"Be my hostess for a House Party I am planning."

"Your hostess?" she said apprehensively.

"You see, since my mother died," he explained, "I have not been able to have mixed parties because there is no one to take care of the ladies. Several of my friends are married and some have grown-up sons and daughters. Welham Abbey used to be famous for its Christmas Ball and I have missed it these past five years."

"House Party and a Ball," she said with sparkling eyes, "Of course I should love it, but I am no Countess, my lord, and the magnitude of the task is breathtaking. Your friends will be very high-ranking I make no doubt." She began to look a little anxious. "I don't think I could do it," she ended doubtfully.

His lordship, who privately thought that she would make a delightful Countess, said consolingly, "It will be quite a small House Party, I am inviting Lord and Lady Fairfield with their son and daughter, and the Earl and Countess of Braye with their daughter. Ivor and Freddy will remain of course and fortunately my sister and her husband are already engaged elsewhere."

"Fortunately, my lord?" she asked, diverted.

"Yes," he said laughing, "My dear sister Janice, who is the most dissatisfied person I know."

"You know I always longed for a brother or sister, someone to share things with," she said wistfully.

"Janice never shared a thing in her life and always resented what other people had as well."

"How sad," said Anne. "She must be unhappy all the time."

"With no good reason since she has a fine man for a husband and two delightful rogues for sons. But we stray from the point. Can I invite my friends and enlist your help?"

Reluctantly at first and then by dint of Lord Welham's persuasion she was brought round to agreeing, and left him, to think over what would need doing, in the privacy of her sitting-room.

Part of Lord Welham's reason for holding the House Party was to introduce Anne gradually into society again. He had realised with shock that she had never had a come-out since she had been married virtually from the school-room. He intended that she should taste the delights of the London Season in the Spring and thought that to revive the Welham Christmas Ball would be a good way to prepare her for that.

After a small lunch Anne decided to take a walk along the back terrace and through one of the formal gardens. Three weeks of confinement to the house, on his lordship's orders, had made her restive and as the day was fine she was tempted out. The terraces and walls were laid out in fine white limestone slabs which were a startling contrast to the dark green juniper trees. Severely trimmed hedges and little beds of still flowering heather made a colourful display even in November. Anne found shelter from a sharp wind on a wooden seat surrounded on three sides by a tall hedge and looked across the geometrical flower beds to a bank of copper beech trees by an old red sandstone wall.

Lord Stone's voice made her jump and ended her reverie. "May I sit down beside you out of the wind?" She nodded and smiled at him.

"Did you know that Lord Welham is holding a Christmas House Party?" she asked.

"He has just told me and I look forward to it very much." He saw her troubled frown and added, "Please call on me for any help that you may need. I have been visiting Welham since I was ten years of age and know it very well."

"Thank you, Ivor, you are very kind," Anne said, laying her hand on his arm. He covered her hand with his and said, "It is not a kindness, Anne, just a desire to smooth your path whenever I can."

She pulled her hand from under his gently and said, "You are my dear friend, Ivor, and I value you for that." She had seen the light in his eyes and was in great fear of hurting him, a thing that she had no wish to do. Ivor could not be put off however. He had been a confirmed bachelor for thirty-five years, stating often that he left it to his brother to continue the line, as he had no wish to be leg-shackled to any woman of his acquaintance. In one month he had changed his mind completely.

"I could be more than your dear friend, Anne, and you know it. Can you give me an answer, my dear?" He possessed himself of her hand and kissed her fingers.

"Oh Ivor, I wish you had not asked me, for I have valued your friendship and restfulness. I must answer you no, and now I suppose I shall lose you completely. Although I love you dearly it is as a brother and that is not the love that you want." She pulled her hand from his again and he saw tears shining in her eyes.

"Please do not cry for me, Anne. The last thing I wish to do is upset you. How can you lose me since I love you and will always do so. If it is a friend you want that is what I will be." She saw the hurt in his eyes and wondered if he knew what he was saying. Swallowing her tears she said lightly, "I am glad you will stay my friend. I do not think I shall ever marry again for my first marriage was not a success. So I shall need a reliable, good kind friend." She rose to leave him and said, "It will be our secret if you wish it." He nodded, not trusting himself to speak again.

Anne went quickly to her sitting-room and wept quietly for the hurt she had unwittingly given Ivor. Liza found her there and going to her put her arm around her and said consolingly, "What is it my dear, tell Liza and perhaps it will help."

"Oh Liza I have hurt a dear friend and I could not help it. How could I tell that he was falling in love with me when all I wanted was his friendship. There is no way to tell a man you do not love him without hurting him, is there?" She wept more tears of remorse.

"Was it Lord Stone, my dear?" Liza said helpfully. "If so you need not fear that he will be unkind."

"But that is worse. He will be very kind and I shall feel dreadful."

Liza smiled at her, "I have no wish to rob you of your triumph, Madame, but I think that in six months time he will secretly be glad that you said no."

Anne looked at her in surprise for a moment, then smiled through her tears. "Freddy said he was a confirmed bachelor." She gave a little gurgle of laughter. "You are very naughty, Liza, to suggest it, but I think you may be right."

The two young girls smiled at each other and Anne dried her tears. "I feel much better already."

"Of course, to be the only lady that Lord Stone ever proposed to is certainly a feather in your cap," Liza said in a satisfied voice.

"I can never tell anyone however," Anne said thoughtfully.

"But *we* know, Madame," Liza said with triumph. She intended to tell her mother at the earliest opportunity. She found that to have a mistress who was sought after by eligible young men gave her a certain vicarious pleasure. Perhaps she would tell Ned, the second groom, with whom she was at present walking out.

The guests had been invited for the third week in December and that gave Anne barely three weeks to prepare for them. She made copious lists of the amounts of food, candles, bed and table linen and other household items that would be needed in excess of those already used. With Mrs. Porter she visited the linen closets and crockery stores to choose what should be used by the guests and their servants. She left Mrs. Porter to delegate rooms to the various valets and ladies-maids and set about an inspection of the upper rooms to choose the best for Lord Welham's guests. She found that not knowing the people concerned made it very difficult to decide what would suit them.

One rainy, windy morning at the beginning of December she sought out Freddy and found him in Lord Welham's gun-room. "Just the person I wanted to see," she announced from the doorway, "I am sure you can help me, Freddy."

"At your service, Madame," he said bowing deeply, "Only come to a warmer room; it is far too cold for you in here."

"Freddy, you treat me like a delicate flower and I am nothing of the kind." She led the way to the drawing-room and seated before a roaring fire put her questions to him.

"You know the people that Lord Welham has invited for Christmas, don't you, Freddy? Tell me about them please."

"What do you want me to tell you?" Freddy asked puzzled.

"How can I choose a room for them when I don't even know how old they are," she protested. "Tell me about Lord and Lady Fairfield and their children."

"Lord and Lady Fairfield," said Freddy thoughtfully. "Well, he is a little older than us, I mean Oliver, Ivor and I. He must be over forty, but he is a cracking rider to hounds. He's a Melton Man, you know. That's where we met him first, when we went to Oliver's estate in Leicestershire."

"A hunting man and nothing else, I see," Anne said, "And his wife?"

"Lady Fairfield is a peevish sort of woman, always creating about something," Freddy looked at Anne and grinned mischievously, "I'll bet I know why she is coming. Her daughter Felicia had her come-out this year, she'll be on the catch for Oliver."

"Freddy," Anne said laughing.

"Not a word of a lie, my dear, every match-making Mama has been on the catch for Oliver for the last ten years or more. I get off easier as I am not yet an Earl."

"Stop it or you'll give me the giggles," she said protestingly. "What about their son? Matthew is it?"

"Oh him," said Freddy scornfully, "A proper little coxcomb he is. Made a cake of himself in town this Spring, dangling after Lord Maybury's wife and writing sonnets to her. Maybury just laughed and said his wife read them to him when he was feeling bored."

"Oh, how unkind of them."

"Not unkind at all. Everyone knows Maybury and his wife are on the best of terms; he was lucky Maybury didn't punch him on the nose."

"But he had no need to tell everyone had he?"

"Since everyone knew what young Fairfield was up to, I suppose he wanted to make sure they also knew that his wife was a respectable woman. There's a lot of gossip goes on in town, you know. You have to be careful you don't become one of the 'on-dits' that the prattlemongers spread about."

"I see, it was the same in Oxford. You were forever hearing scandalous tales about quite respectable people. Tell me about the Earl and Countess of Braye."

"George Braye is really a friend of Oliver's father, though somewhat younger than him. He is a man of considerable intellect and has letters after his name. Do you know, he has written two books on the Civil War, and a learned treatise on William the Conqueror? He also rides well, though not as well as Fairfield." He paused for a moment. "His wife, well, I don't like Lady Braye at all. She is one of those imperious women who look down their noses at you. I always feel as if I have a spot on my cravat or a hair out of place when she looks at me." He smiled, "Well enough when she isn't here my dear, but to be frank, she terrifies me."

"Then she will terrify me too," Anne said apprehensively, "She sounds just like the Dean's wife."

"She's a match-maker too. Lady Drusilla, her daughter, is a dark beauty and has had three seasons. She has turned down more offers than many girls expect to receive, but her eye is on Oliver, and she lives in hope."

Anne sighed and said, "Well, I hope all that will help me to find the right room for them."

"Ask Oliver. He will know."

"I don't wish to ask Lord Welham," Anne said sharply. "This is a job I wish to do alone."

She was destined however to seek Lord Welham's advice about one problem. Although she had been living at Welham Abbey for over two months she was surprised the next day, whilst standing in the hall, to realise that one of the downstairs rooms was unknown to her. As she was deciding whether to leave the oval table in the centre of the hall or move it to one side for better effect, her eyes fell on the door of the room to the left of the entrance. It was at the front of the house overlooking the drive. She went immediately to open it and found that it was locked. She knew that Lord Welham was in his library so she knocked on the door and entered. He looked up from his desk and frowned as she came in. The happy smile faded from her face and she stammered, "I beg your pardon, I am disturbing you," she turned quickly to leave the room overcome with an irrational fear that she had not felt in his presence for some time now. Lord Welham had seen that fear immediately it came and cursed himself for a fool. He hurried to the doors and pulled them open to find her standing at the other side in a daze. He took her hands and pulled her gently into the room, shutting the doors behind her. He spoke softly, "Did you think I was displeased with you, it was my wretched accounts that I was frowning at. Please come and disturb me for I am heartily sick of them."

He led her to a chair by the fire as he spoke and sat her down. "What was it you wanted to tell me?"

She looked up at him and smiled, "You did look rather fierce and stupidly I thought you knew what I wanted. Well, you must have a reason for keeping it locked and perhaps it is private, but it is another room and with guests the more rooms for them to spread themselves into the better, I always think." She drew a long breath after this rather wild speech and looked an enquiry at him.

He smiled back at her and said kindly, "You may think me rather stupid, child, but I am afraid I have no idea which room you mean."

"Oh didn't I say. The one to the left of the entrance; it's locked you see." He looked beyond her for a moment, then said slowly, "Yes, it has been locked since my mother died."

"I am sorry. I should have asked Porter. It doesn't matter, my lord, you have many other rooms." She started to rise from her seat miserable with guilt at disturbing his memories of his mother, but he put his hand on her shoulder and said, "It was a foolish wish I had to preserve her memory. She has been gone for five years and the musical instruments in that room have never been touched since." He smiled at her again. "It would not have been *her* wish that they lie there forgotten. Let me get the key and we will open the door together."

The room had been beautiful before it had been locked

up. The red, chinese-silk wall-cloth was faded and peeling, and the gold window drapes were dingy and limp. The room was large, with an ornate ceiling and a beautiful Adam fireplace. Three large windows overlooked the drive and an elegant archway led to a second room with windows to the front and down one side where the frontage of the house fell back. In the second room was a harp and harpsichord. Several delicate Queen Anne chairs and two sofas were disposed about the first room as if waiting for an appreciative audience to fill them. The carpets were dusty and the beautiful oak boards badly in need of waxing. Glass-fronted cabinets lined the walls and dimly seen through the filmy glass were exquisite china ornaments.

"Surely those are Meissen. Oh, and those are Sévres," Anne said in awe.

"It was my mother's collection," he said with a catch in his throat. "She would be very angry to see them so neglected."

"Such beautiful rooms," she said wistfully, "And so much light in there for the musicians. I do not play myself but Mama used to have Musical Soirées and I can remember hearing the lovely sounds as I lay in bed at night. It was so comforting."

"Could we clean them up in time?" he asked slowly, "We only have two weeks."

"The walls would have to be stripped," Anne said thoughtfully. "But paper hangings could be got from Oxford in time. New drapes would have to be made but any seamstress worth her salt could make them in a week if she applied herself. Three windows in here and four in there, that makes seven. The ceiling would need careful dusting and the fireplace a good wash. Two days for waxing the floor and the cabinets. I will wash the ornaments myself. Do you know a good tuner who could attend to the instruments?" She turned to his lordship and found that he was looking at her in amazement. "I am sorry," she said contritely, "It's my managing way I know. Perhaps you would rather not have your house disturbed."

"I leave it all in your capable hands, child. Why ever did you think you could not arrange my House Party and Ball?"

"But this is *things*," she explained, "I manage very well with things. People, especially Grand People, rather scare me. I am rather a coward you see. Robin said that things don't answer back that's why. I went to one Battalion Ball with him and he . . . It doesn't matter now though," she said suddenly. "Here is something I can do without making a mess of it."

"Did you make a mess of the Battalion Ball?" he asked gently.

That guarded look came over her face and she said stiffly, "It's all so long ago I have forgotten what happened."

He placed his hand on her shoulders and said, "I will make a bargain with you Anne. You tell me about the Battalion Ball and I will give you *carte-blanche* with this room."

She pulled herself sharply away from him and drew a deep ragged breath. "I will not talk to you about Robin. I don't want to remember." Her voice became shrill. "You loved him, everyone loved him, in Spain and here. It must have been me that was wrong, was bad." She ran to the door and turned, "You can keep your mother's room, I don't want it." She dashed the tears from her eyes and shouted, "She loved him too, he told me. I don't want to remember." He took two strides towards her, but she turned and fled.

Lord Welham put Anne's plans into action and brought in an army of workers to implement them. Nothing he could say however would induce her to step into the room or help in any way. She allocated the rooms to the guests with Mrs. Manning's help and discussed menus with the cook. With one week to go everything was falling into place nicely and Lord Welham sought Mrs. Manning's aid. He took her into his library one morning after breakfast and established her comfortably by the fire.

"Mrs. Manning, I have wanted to discuss Anne with you for some time, but have never found the opportunity. Whenever I mention Robin to her she either closes up or gets into a panic. I know that something dreadful must have happened to her in Spain and that my cousin was to blame. I feel that if she can be induced to talk about it she may feel better and begin to heal inside. Until I met Anne I had believed Robin to be a charming and lovable boy, that I was wrong is obvious and my friends have told me things that they have never spoken to me of before. I am appalled at what I have heard and must believe."

"I never wanted her to marry him," Mrs. Manning said bitterly, "I saw straight away that he was not what he pretended to be. I saw also that he did not love my little girl, she was only part of some scheme he had. I talked to Professor Rydal but he was taken in too, and his head was always in the clouds over some parchment or other that he was reading. She would not listen to me, so much in love as she was." She put her hand over her eyes.

"I am sorry to upset you, but I wondered if she told you anything when she came back."

She looked at him sharply, "When she came back, my lord, she was like the living dead. No expression on her face and nothing but skin and bone. Mr. Bates handed her over to me and said I was lucky she was still alive so much she had suffered. He would tell me no more as Miss Anne had sworn him to secrecy. There were marks on her body, but her mind was more scarred. She would wake up in the night screaming, sometimes just to open a door suddenly was enough to set her trembling. At first she would not eat and I could not get her to go out, but gradually the fight she has always had in her came back. There were no smiles or laughs though, until she came here. She told me nothing, my lord, and I met the same resistance as you every time I asked her. 'It's all over,' or 'I don't want to remember,' was all she would say. Your two friends have helped her a great deal to get back her self-respect and even her fights with you have helped, my lord.'' She smiled at him. ''I know you fight; that's the way my girl has always been, resentful of authority. When she fights she is getting better.''

''You think she will never tell then?'' he asked.

''That I don't know, my lord, but I wish she would. Like you, I think that to talk of it would ease her mind. She still has self-doubts and the thought of meeting your House Guests has worried her.''

''I will cancel it if you think it would be better for her.''

''No, I think not. She has to meet people some time.'' She looked at him and then asked, ''What is your particular reason for wanting to help her, my lord?''

He looked back at her and said quietly, ''My family has a great debt to repay her, I think, Mrs. Manning. Anything I can do to make her whole and well again must be done, by a Rowley.''

She gave him a wry smile and said, ''Including a broken arm, my lord.''

He looked at her sharply and a little angrily, then controlling himself said, ''I regret that episode deeply Mrs. Manning, but she can be most provoking you know. I did not know then what I know now and have tried ever since to control my cursed temper.''

''Oh, I know well how irritating she can be and she has a temper too, and too much pride. I have been telling her forever that pride is a sin.''

"And I have that fault too?" he said raising his eyebrows quizzically.

"How could you think that I would be so ill-mannered as to point out your faults, my lord," she said smiling.

"Because you remind me of my own nurse who did so often," he said ruefully.

"I am an old woman, my lord, and that little girl is all I have left to love. I loved her Mama too and promised her on her death-bed to take care of Miss Anne. I wish only to find someone who will love and take care of her, when I am gone. She does need to be taken care of because in spite of her courage she is fearful of so many things."

"You have no need to worry on that score, Mrs. Manning, since I will tell you in confidence that she will be loved and cherished even before you are gone." He spoke gravely and did not look at her as he talked.

"Thank you, my lord," she said equally gravely. "You have set my mind at rest."

Mrs. Manning took Anne to task over her reluctance to enter the music room.

"And why will you not, pray?"

"I don't want to talk about it," she said.

"That's no answer," Mrs. Manning replied promptly. "Who is going to wash those figurines I would like to know. My old hands won't hold them, so if you refuse it will have to be Mrs. Porter, though I have no confidence in her not chipping one or two."

"Oh, no, not Mrs. Porter," Anne cried impulsively.

"Who then, Sarah, Becky, Jane?"

"Very well, I will wash the figurines if someone fetches them out for me."

Mrs. Manning knew well that Anne had a special interest in, and love for fine pottery. She pressed home her advantage. "And that someone will probably clash them together or scratch them."

"Nanny, please," Anne said imploringly, "He made a bargain with me, I cannot keep my side of it."

"Foolish pride again, I make no doubt. On both sides too. If he releases you from the bargain you will go in and help, is that it?"

Mrs. Manning left the room and returned some time later with Lord Welham. He entered Anne's sitting-room sheepishly and standing in the centre of it said, "I had quite forgotten I had made a bargain with you. It was foolish of me and I wish you would forget it." He smiled warmly at her. "I do need your help, Anne. We are at a standstill over the fireplace which will not come clean."

"Nonsense, all that is needed is a little soda in the water," she said briskly to hide her embarrassment. "I will see to it right away."

The transformation that had taken place in one week was overwhelming. The ceiling which really needed repainting was looking quite well. The new paper wall-hangings in a soft rose pink patterned with gold were finished, the floor in the second room was shining with four layers of wax and the turkish carpet looked resplendent. The fireplace had not come clean as his lordship said, but Becky and Jane were hard at work with soft brushes and soda water which was doing the trick. The cabinets had been polished and the glass in the doors was sparkling. Anne had a basin of hot soapy water on an old table and taking one ornament at a time she washed them carefully. The window drapes would arrive in two days and the chairs and sofas were drying out in the servants' quarters where they had been taken, under Anne's supervision, to be carefully sponged and the woodwork cleaned and polished.

Ivor after inspecting the work went to have a word with his friend in the library.

"I am sure she is working too hard," he said.

"She is enjoying herself," Oliver replied.

"She is not yet very strong."

"Mrs. Manning says it is doing her no harm."

"Don't you care that she will be knocked up by all this work she is doing for you?" Ivor said belligerently.

"I would care if I thought it was too much for her," Oliver said tightly.

"I had not noticed your concern," Ivor said scathingly.

"But I have noticed yours, and wonder why you think it should *be* your concern. This is my house and Mrs. Rowley is under my care."

"Then take care of her." By this time Ivor was incensed, an attitude so unusual in him that it surprised his old friend somewhat.

"Hold hard, Ivor. I have no wish to fight with you. What has got into you to make you so angry with me?"

Ivor sat down abruptly and looking at his friend said, "I love her you see, Oliver."

Oliver sat down too and said carefully, "Does she know, have you told her?"

"Oh yes, I have told her. I asked her to marry me some time ago and she refused me. She said she loved me like a brother but did not think that was the kind of love I wanted." He smiled ruefully at his friend and said, "I would have taken her even without love if she would have had me. She told me she would not marry again." He looked away from Oliver who said softly, "I am sorry Ivor. Did you wish to go away, I could find an excuse for you."

"No!" Ivor said sharply, "She wants me for a friend, therefore she will have me."

Oliver stood up and walked over to the window. With his back to the room he said, "How lucky you are, Ivor. She will not have me, even as a friend."

"You too, Oliver?" Ivor said with surprise.

"Yes, me too," his friend replied. "That irritating, aggravating child with a will of her own and a temper to match mine. I dare not even ask her, for I know what her answer would be and I have no wish to see scorn in her sparkling eyes, or hear derision from her lips. Twice I have held her in my arms and I only wish I could do so again." He turned from the window with a laugh and said, "But I have her word for it that she is not used to swoon." His wish was to be granted however in a most unusual way.

Two days later the drapes had not arrived and Anne was getting worried.

"All our work will have been for nothing if they do not come," she said to Mrs. Manning.

"There is nothing you can do but wait," replied her nurse calmly.

Anne stood for a moment and then said, "I shall go and see why she has not finished them."

"Do you think you should?" Mrs. Manning asked anxiously.

"Why should I not?" Anne replied determinedly, "It is not far and I have my pony-trap."

The drapes were being made by a woman who had been recommended to them by the squire's wife. She lived six or seven miles away in Swinford which was a small market town. Anne ordered the pony-trap brought round and accompanied by Liza set out for Swinford. Only half an hour later Lord Welham learned of her journey from Mrs. Manning.

"Gone in the pony-trap to Swinford," he said angrily, "And I was not informed." He rang the bell for Porter who entered the small dining-room where luncheon was laid out. Mrs. Manning prudently kept silent whilst Lord Welham questioned Porter. That august gentleman was not aware that his lordship was not informed of the trip and told him so. When his lordship learned that Anne had only Liza for company he rated Porter soundly for not sending Francis, and Porter reminded him that there was only room for two passengers in the trap, Ned the second groom was driving however so the two young women would be quite safe. Porter withdrew, after a few more words with Lord Welham, in a dignified manner and Ivor said, "No harm can come to them surely, Oliver?"

"There was no need for her to go. Mrs. Porter could have gone." He turned sharply to Mrs. Manning, "Why did you let her go?"

Mrs. Manning said calmly, "Do you think she will come to any harm, Lord Welham?"

"There is a prize-fight in Swinford today. All the riff-raff of the neighbourhood will be there. Who knows what may happen."

Freddy leapt to his feet immediately, "We had better go after her, Oliver."

"I have ordered a carriage round. I shall go myself and bring her back." He left the room in a very bad humour, which did not bode well for Anne when he finally came up to her.

Ivor, Freddy and Mrs. Manning waited for two hours before the sound of carriage wheels on the drive informed them of the return of Lord Welham. They all came out into the hall in time to see Anne enter with a flourish.

"I am quite safe as you see," she said in a brittle voice, "Leave the drapes there and come along, Liza." She turned to go upstairs and Lord Welham coming in after her said icily, "I should like to speak to you in my library, Mrs. Rowley. Now!"

Anne turned sharply about and said in a voice of surpressed fury, "What you said in Mrs. Spriggs' shop was more than I wanted to hear, my lord. I have no desire to have another peel rung over me by someone who has no right to censure me. Just be thankful that I at least remembered my manners and did not upbraid you in public." Mrs. Manning went forward to put a hand on her arm and restrain her but Anne brushed her aside and followed the already departing Liza.

Ivor put out a hand to restrain his friend but he too was brushed aside as Lord Welham bounded up the stairs after Anne.

"Leave them, my lord," Mrs. Manning said quietly, 'They *will* fight but Lord Welham will not harm her."

"He had better not!" Freddy said so belligerently that even Ivor smiled.

Anne handed her pelisse and bonnet to Liza as the sitting-room door flung open by Lord Welham.

"Thank you, Liza, that will be all," she said tightly.

Liza left thankfully and as the door closed behind her Lord Welham said heatedly, "You feather-brained child, did you think I rode all the way to Swinford for no reason?"

"No doubt you had your reasons, my lord, but they are of no interest to me. I do not need a chaperone to ride seven miles."

"There was a prize-fight in that town today and you should not have gone alone."

"I was not alone, I had Liza with me. You shamed me in front of Mrs. Sprigg. You spoke of me as if I was a child which I am not." She turned her back on him and went to the fireplace.

"Then do not behave like a child," he said coldly.

"How dare you speak to me like that," Anne said swinging round, "I am a married lady and in Spain I was used to going to the market every day alone."

"We are not in Spain now however and I have no desire for anyone living under my protection to go about like any hoyden."

"My lord, you forget yourself," she said passionately, "My behaviour today was completely respectable and you know it. I do not, nor will not, ask your permission before I go out. You are not my guardian and never will be. That is the only reason you are angry, because I did not ask you first. But if you think I lower your stock the solution is simple, I shall leave tomorrow morning." She turned her back on him again.

Lord Welham, now thoroughly enraged, strode over to her and swung her round to face him. "Do not turn your back on me when I am speaking to you," he shouted. "You will not leave here tomorrow or any time, nor will you leave these grounds without your footman. The manners you learned in Spain will not do for England."

She took a step back from him and gasped, "I do not wish to hear any more. Leave me alone, you are not a gentleman." She turned and ran to the bedroom door, then shouted wildly, "Leave me alone," before throwing open the door and running through it.

Lord Welham stared into the fire and cursed himself once again for frightening her. "Fool, fool, fool," he said to himself, then more calmly, "If only she would let me take care of her."

Anne refused steadfastly to come down to dinner that evening, and even Mrs. Manning who had been sent by his lordship could not move her. "Tell them I have a headache," she said tearfully, "I cannot sit opposite to that brute and eat. Indeed I do have a headache, he has given me one."

"More likely you have given yourself one through getting into one of your rages," Mrs. Manning said tartly.

"You are always on his side, Nanny," Anne said petulantly. "Go away and leave me alone."

"If that is an example of your manners this evening then it would be better if you did not come down," Mrs. Manning said severely and left her to herself. Food was sent up to her which she refused to eat and finally from boredom she retired to bed quite early.

The first spattering of rain on the windows did not wake Anne nor did she hear the first distant rumbling of thunder. The storm proceeded towards Welham Abbey growing in intensity as it came. Jagged streaks of lightning lit up the whole sky and the first really loud clap of thunder jerked her awake and upright in one searing rush of panic. Since she had been a tiny baby thunderstorms had terrified her and thrown her into hysterical confusion. She put her hands over her mouth to suppress the scream that rose to her lips then groped with one hand for the matches to light her candle. They were not there! Where were they? Another blinding flash followed instantly by a reverberating clash of thunder brought her out of bed. "Nanny, Nanny," she moaned, "It's dark, oh Nanny." She reached her bedroom door and jerked it open as a third flash and bang made her scream. She covered her mouth again to hold it in and started down the corridor. "It's dark, so dark! I can't find you, Nanny. Please God don't let it come again," she muttered with her hands pressed hard against her mouth. The fourth shattering thunderclap released the hysteria that was bubbling up inside her. She fell against the wall, knocked over a small table and rolled herself into a tight whimpering bundle outside the door to Lord Welham's bedroom.

That gentleman had also awoken at the first crash of thunder, and knowing that sleep would be impossible until the storm passed, had lit his candle and sat up in bed. At the third flash he had heard a sound that could have been a scream. Getting up instantly he put on his dressing-gown. Anne's second scream and the upsetting of the table brought him to his door and throwing it open he saw the pathetic weeping bundle on the floor at his feet. He gathered her into his arms and picking up his candle carried her back to her room. He was surprised that the room was in darkness, but as he entered another loud crash made the girl in his arms quiver with terror. He sat on the bed and holding her tightly stroked her hair and spoke soothing words to her whilst the storm raged. Each time the lightning flashed she buried her face in his chest and trembled uncontrollably. At last, and inevitably, the storm passed and as the last thunder rolls became almost inaudible he spoke to her.

"Come, child, it is all over now and you are safe," he said gently. He continued to stroke her hair softly and as the trembling in her body ceased she lifted her head cautiously and looked about her.

"My lord," she whispered, "is this my room?"

"It is your room," he said. "Where did you think you were?"

"I thought I had left it," she said puzzled.

"You did and I brought you back."

"Oh dear, did I wake you? I tried not to scream. I am so sorry." She looked up at him and he smiled at her and said softly, "Where were you going, child?"

"I was trying to find Nanny, but it was so dark."

"Why did you not light your candle?" he asked curiously.

"I could not find the matches you see," she said. "But I remember now I put them on the mantlepiece before getting into bed."

"Why?"

"Because then I would not be tempted to light my candle of course."

"Would that be very bad then?" he asked gently and saw the flush come into her cheeks.

"I am all right now, my lord," she said nervously. "You can go back to bed." She tried to sit up and free herself from his restraining arms, but Lord Welham liked the position he found himself in and was also intrigued by the unlighted candle.

"Lie still, child," he said firmly but kindly. "You have had a severe shock and to rest quietly afterwards is the best thing."

Since she could not free herself and still felt terribly weak Anne ceased struggling and said, as much to change the subject as anything, "I have always been afraid of thunderstorms you see, I expect you think me silly, but indeed I cannot help it. I did try not to scream," she added.

"I know you did," he said smiling, "You pressed your hands over your mouth. He looked down at her and repressed an urgent desire to kiss her. "It is not at all silly. My own mother was a very brave lady, but she was terrified of thunder and I have often comforted her in the night, just as I am comforting you."

"Was she really?" Anne asked in a shaky voice. "Or are you just saying that to make me feel better?"

"Really and truly." He stroked her hair gently then said deliberately, "But she always lit her candle." Her body quivered and holding her tightly again he said, "Tell me why you put your matches over there and why you did not want to light yours." He felt her draw in a shuddering breath before she spoke.

"I am also afraid of the dark, my lord." She twisted her head away from his gaze and said tearfully, "You see what a shocking coward I am, so many things I am afraid of. If I put my matches over there I am not tempted to light my candle if I wake up at night. It is to try and cure me you see."

"And do you think it will?" He took her chin in his hand as he spoke and turned her face towards him. Her lips trembled as she said, "Robin said it would."

"My mother was afraid of the dark also," he said reflectively. "She had a candle burning in her room all night, every night of her life. Everyone who lived here knew that and also knew that they too could have a lighted candle if they wished, be they the lowest scullery maid. Those were my mother's orders.'' He looked at her face still held in his hands. "Robin knew," he said. He watched the tears gather in her eyes and run down her cheeks. They were warm on his fingers as they touched them. "Were you afraid when Robin was with you?" he asked gently.

"No, not when Robin was there," she said tearfully, "Only to be alone in the dark."

"How often was he away then?"

Her face gave her away, as quick pain darted across her eyes. "I don't remember," she said.

"You do," he said gently. "He was away a lot I think."

She pulled her face away from his hand and buried it in his chest. He stroked her hair and spoke softly to her through the sobs that were shaking her body. "You must tell, child, you must. If he was there you did not need a candle, and if he was not there why did you not light one? He would not know, would he?"

Anne lifted her head slowly and looked up at him vaguely. "It is to try and cure me, Robin said." Her voice was barely audible.

"But he would not know," he said again. "Tell me Anne, would he know?"

"By the mark he made," she whispered. "Please, my lord, let me go." She twisted her head from side to side distractedly.

He held her close again and stroked her hair. "What did he do when he found you had used the candle?" He felt her beginning to tremble again and said quietly, "Did he beat you?"

She pushed her hands hard into his chest until he partially released her. "I beg you not to ask me, I cannot tell *you*."

"You can tell me anything about Robin and I will believe it." He took her face in his hands and spoke firmly to her. "I am not trying to hurt you and it is not idle curiosity, only a great desire to help you. There is a great deal of pain in you still and it will remain until you release it. Tell me, child, for I already know of his wickedness and no longer love him."

"I—I—cannot think clearly. What did you ask me?"

"The candle, if you burned it in the night," he said gently.

She pushed his hands away and covered her face with her own hands. "Wasteful, he said, we cannot afford it, I will put a mark, leave the matches over there, that will cure you, or if it does not I will." She took her hands from her face and said sadly, "It was only three times in two years, three times when I could bear it no longer. He b-beat me with his belt, in the morning when he came home to change." She sagged against him and he cradled her in his arms again.

"Where did he go every night?"

"No—No!" she cried vehemently into his chest.

He put his hand under her chin again. "Yes," he said with finality, "You must tell me everything. Where did he go!"

"You are too hard, my lord," she whispered, "And I am too weak. These were my secrets, never to be told. If it had not been for the thunderstorm you would not have found me so weak." Tears fell again as she said, "You have made me cry again."

He wiped her tears away and said softly, "I thank God you were not weak or you would not now be here to tell. Do you not know how strong you have been, how you have fought all alone. You are not alone anymore and have more than yourself to rely on now. Trust me, rely on me, Anne.

You have only to tell once and it will be all over, you will be rid of it.''

"I shall never be rid of it for the rest of my life," she said weakly. "The humiliation, the fear, but mostly the shame."

"It was another woman?" he asked.

She sighed deeply. "Yes, Juanita Lespera. Robin had lived with her, had two children by her and people were beginning to talk. His Commanding Officer told him that unless he came back from England with a wife he would be sent to the front." She hid her face in his dressing-gown.

"How did you find out," he asked gently.

"Robin told me of course," her voice was harsh as she continued. "When we disembarked he took me straight to Esta Rosa and then told me all about her. I did not see him for two days, until he came back with Jim Bates. This is my servant, he said, not yours. He gave me a little money and told me I would get no more for a month. Use it wisely, he said, I shall require to be fed well when I do come home." She lifted her face again and said in a quieter voice, "It was not enough. He beat me for the first time one week later because there was no dinner. I could not light the fire you see. Jim Bates showed me how to do it that night when Robin had gone to her."

"Did Bates help you a lot?"

"Whenever he could without Robin knowing. You see, once when Bates fetched the wood in for me Robin found out and he—he—b—beat me in front of Bates." Her lips trembled but she continued, "When Bates had gone he said, 'He won't help you again; he did not like what he saw'." Her voice became a whisper, "But he did when he could. So too did Mrs. Thomas from the next house."

"Why did you not report him?" he asked gently, "His Commanding Officer would have stopped him had he known." He felt her body go rigid, she covered her face with her hands and moaned, "Ah, no, no, no. I can't remember, I don't want to remember." Her voice began to rise as hysteria threatened to overcome her and Lord Welham gathered her to him and buried her face in his chest. He rocked her gently in his arms and said soothingly, "Hush, child, hush. He cannot harm you now; he is dead. Gently, little one, gently."

When her shuddering sobs had ceased he said carefully. "You went to his Commanding Officer and Robin found out. Is that it?" Her sobbing had changed her voice to a harsh whisper as she said, "I never got there, he found me on the parade ground and guessed my mission. He took me home and made me take off my clothes, then he burned me with the irons from the fire." She stared straight ahead as she spoke, as if she was seeing that little house in Esta Rosa again. "He beat me with it when it went cold. Mrs. Thomas found me when he had gone, it seems I was unconscious and she bathed my wounds and put me to bed. I could not walk for three days and Robin did not come back for a week. When he did he said it was a pity I had not died, but if I went to the barracks again he would kill me. I was so afraid, I dare not go again." Dry sobs shook her body, but there were no more tears for her to cry.

Lord Welham wrapped her in a blanket and sat holding her until the dawn came and she was soundly asleep. He did not sleep at all but only sat and held her, thinking over and over again what she had told him of Robin, once a dear, loved cousin, but now only a monster in his eyes.

In the morning Anne wondered if she had dreamed it all for there was no sign of Lord Welham. She *was* wrapped in a blanket however, and her candle *was* burning when she awoke. To her surprise Liza brought her breakfast in bed, on Lord Welham's orders she said.

Anne went into her sitting-room when she was dressed and looked at the ravages of the storm through her window. It was still raining so she could not go out for a walk, but somehow she felt refreshed in spite of this. She thought of what had happened the night before and felt a flush come to her cheeks as she remembered the things that she had told Lord Welham, things that she had shut out of her mind for so long. There were many more things however that she would not tell him. Humiliations too intimate for other ears. Her cheeks were still faintly flushed when Lord Welham entered shortly after, and came over to take her hand. "I thought you might feel a little unsure about meeting me in company this morning, so I had your breakfast sent up."

"Thank you, my lord, it was most kind of you," she said shyly. "And last night you were most kind also. I am mortified that I kept you from your bed for so long." She looked up at him and surprised a look of such tenderness in his face that it confused her. She pulled her hand from his abruptly and walked over to the fire. "You lit my candle," she said in a slightly agitated voice.

Lord Welham pulled himself together and said mock sternly, "And it will be lit every night from now on or I shall be extremely angry with you." He smiled in a friendly way, and she smiled back with relief. She did not know what had confused her about his look, but his friendly smile was normal and she felt comfortable again.

He walked over to her and said seriously, "I am afraid that sometimes I lose my temper and it is a sore trial to me that I cannot control it. When it has happened before you have been afraid of me and now I know why. Believe me when I tell you, child, that I would never strike you, or harm you, in anyway, even in my worst rage. I wish I could tell you that I will never get in a rage with you again, but I cannot promise. Please do not be afraid of me, Anne." He held out his hand to her and she laid hers in it as she said, "I wanted never to tell anyone about what happened in Spain because I have always wondered if it was my dreadful temper that made Robin . . . do what he did." She looked up at him and said with a hint of a smile, "My father used to tell me that I was aggravating, and had a shocking temper too. If you apologise for yours, then I must for mine I think. I have irritated you, have I not?"

"Frequently," he said smiling back. "But never blame yourself for what Robin did to you, ever. I have found out only recently that you are not the first person he has hurt, and I am ashamed that I never guessed before. Can we call truce, Anne? Forget our differences and be friends? If I promise not to tell you what you must do, will you promise to let me know if you wish to go out of the grounds?" She looked at her hand held in his and then at his face. "Well?" he asked, watching her intently.

She blushed under his close scrutiny and pulling her hand from his said quickly, "I am sure I have no desire to quarrel with you, my lord."

FOUR

Mrs. *Manning and Anne stood in the Hall with Lord* Welham, waiting to receive the first house guests. Everything was in readiness and Anne felt well pleased with her arrangements. An easy friendliness had prevailed between Anne and Lord Welham during the past week, with no more serious argument than why she had driven out to visit Mrs. Draper when she must have known it was about to rain. Her reply that she was not a hot-house plant that would wither from a little rain, was not well received by his lordship, but the day was saved by Ivor who informed them that, if they were going to start shouting at each other then he and Feddy would retire to the billiard-room and leave them alone.

Porter admitted Lord and Lady Fairfield who were followed by their eldest son and daughter. Lord Welham performed the introductions and Anne was immediately impressed by the kindness of Lord Fairfield, who after punctiliously shaking Mrs. Manning's hand, turned to Anne and said, "I am pleased to meet you at last, Mrs. Rowley. I understand you were not in London before your marriage or we would have been sure to have known you." Lady Fairfield Anne did not like, for that lady had no time for Anne or Mrs. Manning. Lord Welham was her goal and she fawned sickeningly on him. Her daughter Felicia was a fair beauty of eighteen with enormous frightened blue eyes, and Anne felt very sorry for her as she tried to efface herself from her mother's conversation. She is very timid, Anne thought. Poor girl, she would like to be anywhere but here. Anne moved over to speak to her much to Felicia's obvious relief. The Honourable Matthew Fairfield strolled nonchalantly over to join them and Anne, catching Lord Welham's eye at that precise moment, was hard put not to laugh. He was a young coxcomb and his dress was outrageous. Yellow pantaloons were topped by a startling waistcoat and a very blue jacket. His driving-coat had ten capes and threatened to engulf him. High shirt points and a complicated cravat completed his dress and it was obvious that he thought himself a very fine fellow.

"Nice to meet you," he said casually, flicking an imaginary speck of dust from his sleeve.

"If you would follow me," Anne announced, "I will take you to your rooms."

Anne had taken great pains to ensure that every room was warm, comfortable and hospitable. Flowers decorated the ladies' rooms and each gentleman would find a decanter and glasses discreetly disposed in his bedside cupboard. Lord and Lady Fairfield had been given a suite of rooms on the second floor and their daughter a room opposite them in the same corridor. Matthew Fairfield was at the opposite side of the house in a room next to Freddy and Ivor.

"It will not do," Lady Fairfield stated. "I must have my daughter in a communicating-room."

"But she is just across the passage-way, my dear," her husband said placatingly.

"And if she needs me in the night, sir?" his wife demanded. "I must needs across a public corridor to go to her."

Anne thought furiously and came up with a solution that would need a great deal of hard work to accomplish.

"That would be extremely awkward, Lady Fairfield," she agreed. "If you will just leave your things here and come to the sitting-room I will get your servants to transfer your things to better rooms, where your daughter will be next to you." She thought privately that Felicia looked a little disappointed, as she led them to the sitting-room on the first floor.

Half an hour later and looking somewhat flustered she found Freddy and Ivor in the billiard-room.

"I am afraid I have had to dispossess you of your rooms." She sat down suddenly and said. "I do hope you don't mind, but Lady Fairfield was so insistent and I didn't know what to do."

Ivor came to her instantly and sitting beside her said gently, "What has that stupid woman been up to to make you so fussed, my dear?"

"She didn't like her rooms," Anne said wearily, "So I have moved her and Lord Fairfield into yours and Freddy's. She wanted her daughter in a communicating-room and yours, and the one I gave to Matthew, are the only three that connect in the whole house. All of your things have been moved to theirs."

"Good God," Freddy said warily, "does my man know?"

"Yes, for I specially asked him to move yours himself."

"Then you are braver than I," said Freddy ruefully, "Didn't he kick up a dust about it?"

"Not when I told him I would let nobody but him supervise the packing and unpacking of your things, since I knew just by looking at you what great care he took of you." She smiled at Freddy and added, "He is quite amenable really. I wonder at you being so in awe of him."

"Anne, you are a complete hand," Ivor said laughing, "Even Oliver is careful how he approaches Freddy's man."

"Well you may laugh, Ivor, but your man looked a trifle put out at my request until I told him that Freddy's man was personally supervising his master's packing. He jumped to with a will then, not wishing to be thought backward in his care of you."

Lord Welham entered the billiard-room and said, "What is this Porter tells me about Lady Fairfield disrupting the whole house?" He glanced speculatively at Anne and saw the tired look on her face. "You do too much, Anne. I had not thought of giving you extra work when I planned this House Party. That tiresome woman would have stayed put if I had been there."

"No she would not, my lord, and well you know it. The hospitality of Welham Abbey was at stake. I have done nothing except to tell the servants what rooms to carry their things to."

"Well, that's a plumper to start with," Freddy said good-humouredly, "You have wheedled my man shamefully and that would be enough to tire me out for a whole week."

Oliver smiled at her. "Porter told me what you said to Freddy's man. I rather gather that you have impressed my butler immensely." He pulled her to her feet and said, "Now you will rest in your room until it is time to dress for dinner."

"But the guests," she protested.

"Will be entertained by Freddy, Ivor and myself."

At her mulish look he said lightly, "You surely do not delude yourself into thinking that Lady Fairfield is pining for your company do you?"

Her look became a smile as she replied, "Nor I for hers, my lord, but Felicia is different. I would not desert her, for she is frightened of her Mama you know, and of you I think.''

His brows drew together and he said sharply, ''She has no need to be afraid of me; I am no danger to her. She is too insipid by far for my taste.''

Anne pulled her hand from his and said bitingly, ''You are not to her taste either, my lord, but rather to her Mama's. There is no need to frown at her when her Mama makes her speak to you, however, a kind word would put her at her ease.''

''Which is precisely what I do not wish to do,'' he answered, ''in case her Mama misunderstands it.'' He saw her eyes flash and said, ''Peace, peace, child. I will get Ivor to entertain her for you. Will that do?''

''Will you, Ivor?'' she asked anxiously. He smiled at her and said, ''I will, if you will go and rest.'' Anne retired thankfully.

The next day saw the arrival of the other house guests and the party was complete. Lord Braye shook Anne's hand, mentioned her father and retired to Lord Welham's library to answer a letter he had received that morning from his publisher. Lady Braye inspected her minutely from head to foot, obviously found her wanting, and dismissed her from her mind. Lady Drusilla was falsely sweet, and under cover of fond greeting, inspected Anne in much the same way that Lady Braye had done. Drusilla was the most beautiful girl that she had ever seen. She was the same age as Anne and slightly tall for a woman. Her dark lustrous hair was dressed in the height of fashion and her creamy skin, luminous eyes and delicately curved lips all added to a picture of loveliness that Anne found breathtaking. Her greeting of Oliver was as one friend to another, but Anne noted with interest that Oliver's greeting lacked the warmth of Drusilla's. She remembered what Freddy had told her of that young lady's hopes, and found it remarkable that Lord Welham was not in love with her.

At dinner that evening Anne was seated in the hostess's place opposite to Lord Welham. It was obvious that Drusilla viewed this situation with displeasure. The fact that Anne, by virtue of being a married lady, preceded her was not to her liking either and she showed it. When the gentlemen joined them in the drawing-room after dinner Anne was heartily thankful. Mrs. Manning who had been introduced as Anne's companion was ignored by Lady Fairfield who considered herself above such people. Lady Braye however, a much cleverer woman, had held Mrs. Manning in conversation with the object of finding out about Anne. Nanny was more than a match for the Lady Brayes of this world and told only what she wished that exalted lady to know. She dwelt at length on the lineage of Anne's Mama and on her Papa's well-bred connections. Lady Fairfield was reciting a homily to her daughter in undertones and Anne was perforce thrown upon Drusilla's untender mercy. That young lady turned her luminous eyes on Anne and with a shock Anne saw in their depths a hardness and cruelty that was not unknown to her. She felt a shiver pass through her and only dimly heard what Drusilla was saying.

"I beg your pardon," Anne said, "did you ask about Spain?"

"I asked where you had lived," Drusilla said.

"In Cadiz," Anne replied mechanically, "On the Via Ventura."

"I was very surprised when I heard that Robin had married you. It was sudden was it not?"

"To me, no. Robin had been at Oxford before he went to Cadiz you know. We merely resumed our acquaintance when he returned." Anne spoke quietly and uninterestedly but Drusilla was not to be stopped. "But you were only sixteen when you married."

"I would prefer not to talk of Robin if you don't mind, Lady Drusilla, it is only just over a year since he died."

"Do you mean to tell me that you were in love with him," Drusilla said in a soft voice. "If so I am afraid that I don't believe you. Robin was cruel and bad, nobody could love him for long." Drusilla smiled a cruel smile at Anne who got up and walked over to join Mrs. Manning and Lady Braye. She felt acutely uncomfortable in Drusilla's company and could feel panic welling inside her as that young lady also rose and came over to join them. Fortunately for her the gentlemen joined them at that moment and Freddy came over to speak to her. His gently shy smile and mute appeal reminded her that he too was nervous and needed her help.

*Drusilla, Lady Braye and the gentlemen rode most morn*ings and as Lady Fairfield was a late riser, Anne found herself often in Felicia's company. After enjoying a quiet breakfast together they would walk in the gardens when the sun shone, or in the long gallery if the weather was bad. Anne found in Felicia all of the things she had always wanted in a sister and very soon they were on first-name terms with each other. Felicia was a quiet gentle girl who, whilst not having the learning that Anne had acquired from her father, was by no means a dunderhead. She was an extremely able musician and could discuss music and composers with ease. She also shared with Anne a talent for water-colour painting and a love of art and fine ornaments that gave them ample scope for conversation. Their friendship blossomed under Lord Welham's watchful eye and he found himself in charity with Felicia Fairfield for the first time. It had not escaped his notice that Drusilla was less than kind to Anne, or that Anne was not comfortable when talking to Drusilla. Felicia's friendship for her made it easier for him to entertain his gentleman guests without wondering what Anne might be doing.

As Christmas Day came nearer the weather improved with crisp frosty mornings, and a watery sunshine in the afternoons. Anne had been kept busy for two days writing out invitations for the Christmas Ball. It was to be held in the first week of the new year at the full moon. Those guests who lived nearby would be returning home in the small hours when a bright moon would be necessary for safe driving. Those from further afield would stay the night and return the next afternoon. When the replies came back, bedrooms would have to be allotted to those guests who would be remaining, and as some of those rooms had not been used for five years there was a lot of preparation to be got underway.

Anne was seated alone in her sitting-room one afternoon, busy with the invitations, when a knock on her door caused her to lay her pen down. Lord Welham entered and frowned when he saw the pile of cards on her bureau.

"Could not Mrs. Porter do those?" he asked.

"Well she could, my lord, if you wish your guests to get a splotched invitation," she said smiling at him.

"You have an answer for everything," he said still frowning.

Her smile faded and she said anxiously, "I am sorry, my lord, but her writing is not good you know."

He looked at her quickly and banished his frown abruptly, "I am sorry that you thought I was censuring you Anne, I was not, only the amount of work that I have heaped on your shoulders. I had no idea that it needed this much effort to arrange a Ball."

"But I enjoy it," she said brightly, "Though I must confess that my hand will not write any more this afternoon. Also I am promised to Felicia for a walk whilst her Mama rests. Will you not join us, my lord?''

''Willingly, except that I am also promised to Lord Braye, who wishes to discuss some point of his new book with me. Perhaps I will join you later.''

''I don't suppose you will,'' Anne said with a smile, ''When gentlemen discuss their latest book they lose all count of time.''

As Anne and Felicia descended the steps of the south terrace they encountered Freddy, who urged by Anne, agreed to join them. They passed under the archway in the old wall and entered the sheltered garden. Freddy offered an arm to each young lady and they strolled down the ancient flagged path between tall old hedges. It was a winter garden and many plants and shrubs gave it a subtle, muted colour. Anne stopped by one that had leaves that looked like silver, and was surprised when Felicia was able to tell her its name.

''Do you know the names of all the plants?'' Freddy asked surprised.

''Well, not precisely all of them,'' Felicia answered shyly, ''But I do know a great many of them.'' She demonstrated her talent by naming a few more and Anne said, ''You must have studied Botany, Felicia.''

''I have not studied it,'' Felicia said, ''but I have many books on the subject and Papa allowed me to experiment at home. Mama does not consider it precisely ladylike but Papa says I have made the gardens more interesting.'' She turned an animated face towards her companions and added, ''And I do enjoy it so much.''

''Well, I call it jolly clever,'' said Freddy, ''I do like a nice garden, but I have no idea how to achieve one. Our gardener is so old that he won't change anything.''

''How tiresome for you,'' Felicia replied without a trace of shyness. ''Will your father not pension him off?''

"I've a good mind to put it to him when I go home," Freddy said also without any trace of shyness.

Anne prudently kept silent and watched happily as the two friends talked to each other. When they reached the end of the garden Felicia had persuaded Freddy to come and see Lord Welham's fine rose garden. With great tact Annie insisted that she must return to her invitation writing and left them passing through to the rose garden. She turned and retraced her steps, well satisfied with her little ruse and wondering why it had never occured to her to throw them together before. They were so well suited to each other.

On returning to her sitting-room Anne set about writing the invitations once more. Some time later she was disturbed by a knock on her door and thinking it was Lord Welham called out, "Come in," and continued writing. A soft honeyed voice that she knew well addressed her.

"I have wanted the opportunity for a few private words with you, Mrs. Rowley. Will you please stop pretending to be busy and listen to me."

Anne turned in surprise to see Drusilla's beautiful face twisted in scorn.

"This is my private sitting-room and you have no right to be in here," Anne said defensively.

"You invited me in," Drusilla replied, "It is just the place for a private conversation."

Anne stood up with a resolution she was far from feeling.

"Say what you have to say, then go," she said.

"Oh I intend to," Drusilla drawled, "but I shall leave when I am ready." She moved nearer to Anne and continued, "You are a little afraid of me I think and so you should be. I can be just as cruel as Robin when it is necessary." She smiled maliciously as Anne stepped back from her and said falteringly, "I don't know what . . . Why are you here?"

Drusilla walked across the room and seated herself before the fire. Raising her beautiful luminous eyes to Anne's apprehensive face she said crisply, "I do not know by what insinuating ways you have managed to foist yourself upon Oliver, but I can tell you now that he is mine." Anne opened her mouth to speak but Drusilla stopped her. "I have no desire to hear what you have to say, only listen to me and mark my words well. I have seen you smiling at him and I warn you that if you make any attempt to take him from me with your languishing airs I shall make quite sure that you are stopped. I have many friends who would be only too happy to prove to you how wrong you are being. Friends who have the same tastes that Robin and I have." She paused to gauge Anne's reaction to this statement and was gratified by the pallor that she saw on her face. "Good, I see that you understand me," she said rising. "Remember well, Mrs. Rowley, I shall be watching you." Her cruel eyes sparkled dangerously as she passed Anne and left the room.

Anne sat down and tried to stifle a desire to burst into hysterical tears. What does Drusilla mean? she thought. What languishing airs? Does she think that I wish an alliance with that man, or indeed that he wishes one with me? Can she not see that I dislike him intensely? He is a Rowley and just like Robin. Well, perhaps not quite like Robin. Standing up she moved restlessly to the window. How can I stop doing something that I am not doing? she asked herself. Drusilla's cruel eyes came into her thoughts and she shivered slightly. She cannot hurt me here, she thought resolutely. And since I am not on the catch for her precious Earl, I have nothing to fear from her. The remembrance of Drusilla's reference to Robin made Anne shiver again. She supposed that Drusilla must have known him well since she appeared to be very familiar with Lord Welham. No, she would not think about Robin. She had found it easier of late to put him right out of her mind.

When Lord Welham entered her room some time later she was once again busily engaged in writing out invitations. A certain look about her eyes worried him and he took it to be tiredness.

"Have you been here for all of the afternoon?" he asked.

"Not at all," she replied, "I have had a nice walk with Felicia and Freddy."

Coming to her he drew her to her feet. "No more writing today," he said kindly. "You have tired yourself out."

"But the invitations, they must be finished. I wanted them sent out tomorrow."

"Then I will finish them," he said evenly, and in spite of her protestations he gathered them all together with the list and after ordering her to rest before dinner, left the room.

The last minute preparations for the Ball left Anne with no time to worry about Drusilla's threats and indeed she saw little of Lord Welham except at dinner and when the gentlemen rejoined the ladies after the port.

On Christmas day, she received an unusual and private present from him that had been left in her sitting-room. The note on it said only, "I thought that you would feel more comfortable in this at the Ball." It was an extremely elegant London gown.

*Anne sat before her mirror and watched Liza put the fin-*ishing touches to a new and very grand hair style.

"Now, Madame, the Ball gown," she said at last. The shimmering gold satin barely covered Anne's shoulders and a half dress of sheer spider gauze fell from beneath her breast and drifted gently about her whenever she moved.

Delicate gold slippers completed the picture and moved Liza to say reverently, "Oh Madame, you look beautiful."

Anne stared at her reflection and could not help admiring herself, but she shook her head and said, "Beautiful? No, Liza, I don't think so, but you have done my hair beautifully, and I thank you." She rose from her seat and spun round. "Oh Liza, it's so nice to be dressed up again." Her face glowed with pleasure and pink spots shone on her cheeks.

Liza smiled with satisfaction and said, "Go into your sitting-room, Madame, whilst I tidy up in here." She had received explicit instructions from Lord Welham that Anne was to be ready and in her sitting-room half an hour before dinner. "If he doesn't think her beautiful," she thought as she tidied the room, "then he is a fool."

The sitting-room door opened and Lord Welham, resplendent in evening dress, entered. Smiling he said, "You look beautiful Anne, I knew that colour would suit you."

She blushed rosily and answered, "No, not beautiful, my lord, that I could never be. The dress is beautiful however, and I am very grateful to you for it."

"I hesitate to contradict you, child, for it might lead to an argument," he said laughingly, "But to me you look beautiful in that dress. Am I not allowed to say so?" He raised his eyebrows quizzically and smiled his friendly smile at her.

Anne responded to his mood and giving a deep curtsey said in a mannered way, "I thank you, my lord, you are indeed gracious."

Going to her he raised her with one hand. "It lacks but one finishing touch and I have it here." So saying he put his hand into his pocket and brought out a jewel case.

"Good heavens, my lord, another present?" Anne said involuntarily.

He looked at her keenly and said, "It will be your birthday very soon I think, this is an early present." He opened the case to reveal a very fine pearl necklace. To his surprise and dismay Anne took one look at the pearls and burst into tears. She covered her face with her hands and whispered, "Oh, I am sorry, so sorry, please forgive me." He put down the case and going to her turned her about to face him. "Tell me what it is, child, only tell me what it is I have done."

"It is not you, my lord. I am so sorry to spoil your gift like this, so sorry." Fresh tears spilled down her face and he led her to the sofa and sat her down.

Still with his arm about her he proffered his handkerchief and said, "It is Robin again is it not, my dear?"

She dried her tears but fresh ones fell as she answered him, "You always guess do you not? Yes, it is Robin again." He took the handkerchief away from her and wiped away her tears.

"Tell me now, Anne, then you will feel better. I will take the pearls away if you wish it."

"No, it is foolish to care after so long, but it reminded me you see." She looked at him with a rueful smile, then said, "You asked me once to tell you about the Battalion Ball, do you remember?"

"Yes, I remember. Will you tell me?"

"Robin said I must go, His Commanding Officer would expect it. By then the only jewellery I had left was my mother's pearls that she had given to me the day before she died." Her voice became reflective as she continued. "All the others were gone, sold by Robin, even the gold bracelet that my father gave me as a wedding present. There was never enough money for Juanita, she always wanted more and Robin would give her whatever she asked for." She looked up at Oliver for one moment and then looked down at her hands in her lap. "I was even happy to go, Robin was kind and said I looked well, although my gown was sadly out of date. He made me fasten my hair back, however, and I was glad to do so when he said everyone would stare at me if I did not.''

His arm around her shoulder tightened for a moment and he said softly, ''My poor child, such beautiful hair it is too.''

She frowned up at him and said, ''I did not think so then, my lord.'' He saw an abstracted look appear in her eyes as she continued, ''I wore my mother's pearls and felt almost happy, as it seemed that Robin would not hurt me then. *She* was there, one of his friends had invited her. She looked so beautiful with her dark hair and large black eyes, somewhat like Drusilla is, my lord.'' She paused and drew in a ragged breath. ''All went well until half way through the evening when Robin danced with her. After the dance he took me to a small ante-room and told me to take off my pearls as Juanita had seen them and wanted them.'' Tears began to flow again and she spoke in a harsh voice. ''I begged him not to take them. I lost my temper and began to shout, 'You shall not give them to your mistress,' I said, but he caught me by my hair and pulled it hard, then took off the necklace himself. He said that I should not own *things* until I could cope with people. 'No one has danced with you,' he said 'because you are incapable of mixing in society. Until you lose your fear of people you will own nothing.' He took my pearls away, then came back and said that he had told everyone I had the headache. He sent me home in a carriage.'' She sat quite still and Lord Welham did not speak either, until at last to break the silence he said gently, ''And you never saw your pearls again?''

''Oh yes,'' Anne said in a hard voice, ''I saw them the next day when I went to the market. She passed me in a carriage and she was wearing my mother's pearls. I wanted to jump on her and twist them around her throat until she died.'' Anne looked up at Oliver again and said with a wry smile, ''But I couldn't you see because Robin was with her in the carriage. I think he had done it on purpose because they both waved to me as the carriage passed by.'' She shivered and then said, ''You see what a wicked temper I have, my lord. I would have killed her for a string of pearls if Robin had not been there.'' She put her face in her hands and wept again.

Lord Welham could find nothing to say, nothing that could possibly express the bitter feelings that welled up in him. The brutality of his cousin was almost too much for him to bear and had he been a weaker man he would have cried for the girl seated beside him. Instead, taking her tear-soaked face in both hands he spoke to her with great compassion. ''I am not surprised that you wanted to kill her, child, perhaps only your anger saved you from going mad and I am glad of it. Will you accept my pearls until such time as I can return yours to you?''

''Return mine, my lord!'' she said shakily. ''How can you do that? It is more than a year, almost two, since Robin gave them to her.''

''Nevertheless they will be found if my agents have to scour the whole of the Peninsular to find them. You will have them back, Anne.''

She turned her face away from him and said softly, ''If you can find them, my lord.''

''Even if she has sold them they will be traceable, child. It can be done. Trust me, Anne.''

''I believe you mean to try, my lord, but I doubt even your ability to wrest them from her.'' She paused, then said, ''Her triumph was short lived, however, as Robin was sent to the front the next week for his audacity in bringing her to the Ball. I was glad when he went, I hoped he would die. It was not until he did however that I realised how destitute and alone I was. Jim Bates had not gone with

91

him because he was too old and ready to be pensioned off. If it had not been for him I would have starved long before news of Robin's death came through. I used to dream that I would go to her and demand my mother's pearls back, but I lacked the courage. She had cruel eyes too you see.''

He rose from the sofa and fetched the jewel case. Taking the pearls out he clasped them around her neck. They gleamed translucently against her creamy skin and he longed once again to hold her in his arms and kiss her. Instead he said with a smile, ''Pearls suit you, Anne; you make them glow.''

The sound of the dinner gong reminded them both that they had guests. Lord Welham hurried away to attend them, whilst Anne slipped into her bedroom to sponge her face and tidy her hair before going downstairs.

The Ball was an undeniable success and both Anne and Oliver were complimented by the many exalted guests. Oliver watched Anne enjoying herself and found that he was not the only one with an eye upon her. Drusilla's cold stare amused him until he chanced to see her close beside Anne, and caught the look of malevolence that she gave her. Anne's slight recoil and look of fear changed his amusement to anger and he resolved to keep a close eye upon Drusilla for the remainder of her visit.

The end of January saw the departure of the guests and Anne, although much more confident after her first venture into society, was not sorry to bid goodbye to Lady Braye and Drusilla. She had been alarmed at the intensity of hatred that she saw for herself in that young lady's eyes and wondered what she could do to convince Drusilla that far from considering her a desirable partner, Lord Welham found her aggravating and nothing but a child.

The departure of the Fairfields made Anne rather sad as she had found much pleasure in Felicia's company, but when it came time to say good-bye to Ivor and Freddy she received a pleasant surprise. Freddy led her to one side and said quietly, "I mean to apply to Lord Fairfield very shortly and I wanted you to know."

"Oh Freddy, you cannot imagine how happy you have made me," she said delightedly.

"Yes I can," he whispered, "for it has made me very happy too. Felicia is willing, but you must not say anything to Oliver or Ivor, until I know if I am acceptable to her Papa."

"What are you two whispering about?" Oliver said coming over to them.

"Nothing at all," Anne replied and giving him a radiant smile she led Freddy out of the door and down the steps to his carriage.

"Well, if it makes you so happy you may keep your secret," Lord Welham murmured to himself as he followed them out.

FIVE

On a cold February day Anne walked slowly back to the
Abbey across the park. Snowdrops were showing through
beneath the trees and in some of the hedges she had passed,
pussy-willows abounded. Anne had walked further than she
had intended to, but the clear sky after the snow and rain
of January had tempted her out. She hurried as she neared
the house, sure that it was time already for luncheon and
that she would be late. Her anxiety was for Mrs. Manning
who would be worrying about her, for Anne was afraid
that Nanny was not looking well. When she entered the
hall some moments later Lord Welham was crossing to go
up the stairs. He paused and looked at her, then said, "I
was beginning to wonder where you were. Luncheon has
been waiting this past half hour."

Something in his voice worried Anne and she replied
sharply, "Merely a longer walk than I intended, my lord.
I informed Porter where I was going since you were engaged in your library."

"You are free to come and go as you please in the
grounds as you well know, Anne," he said equally sharply,
then coming towards her he said more normally, "It was
just that I had disquieting news whilst you were gone and
wanted to impart it to you myself."

"Nanny," Anne whispered fearfully, "Is it Nanny? I must go to her." She started for the staircase, but Lord Welham stopped her with his hand on her arm.

"Just one moment, child," he said gently. "Mrs. Manning has the influenza and the doctor is with her."

"Let me go to her then," she said urgently.

"No, you must not go to her until the infection has gone," he said holding her back.

"Is that your order, my lord?" she asked angrily.

"No, not my order, Anne, her request and you will obey it."

"I will not," Anne said instantly. "I don't believe you."

"That is your choice," he said coldly, "But you will do as I say nonetheless." She tried to pull her arm from his grasp but was not able to do so.

"You are hurting me," she said tearfully.

"I am sorry for that, Anne, but until you promise not to go to Mrs. Manning's room I shall not release you."

"You are insufferable," she shouted, "It is my Nanny and I love her." She wept tears of frustration. "Let me go."

"Do not shout where all the servants can hear you," Lord Welham said calmly.

"Do not tell me what to do," Anne retorted fiercely.

"Very well, since you behave like a child, I shall treat you like one." So saying he swung her round, picked her up in his arms and carried her up the stairs to her sitting-room. In her room he dumped her unceremoniously on her sofa, shocking Anne into silence and frightening her a little. "Mrs. Manning particularly asked me to keep you from the sick-room until all danger of infection was past," he said sternly.

"But she is ill, she doesn't know what she is saying."

"It would distress her however if I allowed you to go to her and that is the last thing I want to do."

"Is she very ill?" Anne asked plaintively. "Will she die, my lord? Please tell me now if you think so."

"She is very old of course and until the doctor has finished his examination I do not know."

"She nursed me through every illness I had," Anne said softly. "When I came back from Spain I was ill for a long time, and she cared for me so well. I had thought that if she was ever ill I could repay her for all she has done for me. Now I cannot even see her." She looked at Lord Welham suddenly, "Who is nursing her, my lord?"

Happy that her thoughts were diverted he said, "I have sent Liza's sister home and am expecting Mrs. Draper at any moment. She is used to nursing you know, as she cared for my mother during her last illness."

Anne smiled at him suddenly and said, "You are very kind to Nanny, Lord Welham, and I am grateful to you."

"She is a remarkable lady and I am very fond of her," he said smiling back.

"But I am a sore trial to you I know," she said lowering her gaze, "Do you persevere with me just because you like Nanny?"

Lord Welham was struck dumb by Anne's question. How to answer her taxed his brain for a long moment, as he was aware that to declare himself at this time would be foolhardy. Anne looked up surprised by his silence and composing his face into a smile he said lightly, "No, not just for that reason. I have become used to having you here you know and would be sadly dull rattling about in this large house alone."

"It has seemed very quiet since the company departed, hasn't it," she said. "That's why I went for a long walk this morning. I miss having Felicia to accompany me."

"Then perhaps you and I could take a walk together sometimes," Lord Welham said happily, "I too miss Ivor and Freddy when I go riding."

"If you would not find it terribly dull, my lord, I should like that," she answered shyly. "But I should warn you that I do not walk quickly as I like to study nature as I go."

"A favourite topic of mine," he replied promptly.

"Now that I do not believe," she said with a laugh. "No gentleman is interested in nature for itself." She cast him a mischievous grin and continued, "But maybe I can teach the lettered Earl of Welham something that he does not know."

"Then I shall spend the time before our walk in my library reading all I can find on Nature in order not to appear too stupid." A knock on the door interrupted their pleasant conversation and Porter announced the doctor. His news was not unduly grave for he pronounced Nanny remarkably fit for her age. He concurred heartily with Nanny and Lord Welham in their plans to keep Anne from the sick room and with that she had to be content.

A week later Anne, still barred from Nanny's room and desirous of something to do, decided to drive over to Mrs. Draper's house in the village to see if Sarah was coping well with the younger children. Mrs. Draper's second daughter Sarah had been employed at the Abbey in place of Liza as parlourmaid and although she was sixteen Anne thought her very young to be left in charge of the other children. She resolved to ask Mrs. Draper if there were any messages she wanted delivered, then ride over with Liza in the pony-trap. Summoning Francis, who was now her personal footman, she told him her plans and sent him to see Mrs. Draper. Her disappointment was great therefore when Porter informed her that all hands in the stables were engaged in cleaning and whitewashing the entire block. They would be finished before lunch however so if she wished to go in the afternoon all would be well. It fretted her that she could not go when she wanted to, but returning to her sitting-room she encountered Francis. "Oh Francis, I cannot go this morning as there is no one to drive me," she said sadly. "I shall have to go this afternoon."

Francis, a young man of eighteen years, was ardent in his devotion to Anne and her welfare. As personal footman he was one removed from the ordinary footmen at Welham and jealous of his new status, but far outweighing that was a desire to please a mistress whose kindness in the past had endeared him to her.

"I could drive you if you wish, Madame," he replied instantly.

"Can you drive then, Francis?" she asked kindly.

"Yes, Madame, for my brother is head groom to the Squire and he has taught me." Anne was not to know that with the recklessness of youth Francis was overstating the facts. His brother had on several occasions allowed him to move carriages about the stable-yard at the Hall, but Francis had never driven on the open road.

Anne, however, happy to have her predicament resolved, sent him instantly to the stables to procure her pony-trap. By an unhappy chain of events, no one in a position to cry *halt* to their plans was made aware of their intentions. Francis encountered a mere stable-boy, who was glad to lay down his broom and harness the pony to the trap. The head groom and his more responsible staff were all engaged in trying to entice Lord Welham's mettlesome hunter, who had taken exception to the whitewash, out of his stall. When Anne descended to the hall with Liza the door was opened for her by a very young footman who had been left on duty whilst Porter addressed himself strongly to his retinue about their lax behaviour since the departure of the guests. Lord Welham was engaged in his library with the steward from his Leicestershire estates, and Anne passed through the front-door unchecked. Liza attempted to thwart her plans by exclaiming, when she saw Francis in the driving seat, "His lordship would not like you to be driven by Francis, Madame. Ned has told me that the orders to the stables are that only the very best hands are to drive you."

"What nonsense!" Anne replied instantly. "Francis has been taught by his brother who is head groom to the Squire. If however you are too nervous to come with us you may remain here, Liza."

Thus vanquished Liza climbed into the pony-trap and the journey commenced. When they turned out of the drive Anne became instantly aware that Francis was not as expert as he had led her to believe. She commanded him to drive very slowly and he was happy to oblige.

On arriving in the village they were greeted ecstatically by Sarah who was finding two brothers and a sister rather a handful. Liza quickly assessed the situation and gave her sister rapid instructions on exactly how to cope with the young ones. Anne was very diverted with this glimpse into family life and regretted once again being an only child.

On the journey home Anne was very quiet and Liza feared that Sarah had upset her, but when she asked Anne she was surprised at her reply. "No, Liza, not exactly. But seeing Sarah there all flustered and unsure of herself reminded me of when I first arrived in Spain. I was the same age as Sarah and I had no idea what to do, like her. Your home is beautiful of course and cannot compare with my shack on Esta Rosa except in size. I am afraid I was not nearly as competent as Sarah and it's no wonder Robin was angry with me."

To her surprise Liza's face became hard and angry. "There is nothing you can tell me about Master Robin, Madame, that I would not believe." She turned to Anne and compassion replaced anger on her face as she said, "I have said nothing to you about him, Madame, because I just know that you must have suffered greatly at his hands.''

"How do you know that?'' Anne said surprised and dismayed. Surely Lord Welham had not betrayed her confidence to Liza of all people.

"Master Robin was born the same year as I was,'' Liza said tightly. "He came to live here when he was five years old, after his parents died. Because we were the same age we used to play together.'' She paused for a moment, then turning a tragic face to Anne said, "You will not be aware that I had a brother, younger than me by one year. When I was seven and he was six he drowned in the lake. Master Robin took him out in the boat, although we were forbidden to do so. He would not take me and I found out why. In the middle of the lake he pushed Harry out of the boat, then rowed back to the bank and watched him drown. I could do nothing for I could not swim, but Master Robin could, for he had been taught by his lordship.''

"But why, why?'' Anne said in horror, "Did no one find out?''

"Harry had been boxing with him that morning,'' Liza said softly. "He made Master Robin's nose bleed and he said to him, I will get even with you this afternoon, Harry.''

"Did you not tell, Liza?''

"I told my Mama and she told Lord Welham's father, but she insisted that the Countess should not know because she loved her so much. My father was dead and I was told never to speak of it again.''

"And did you not?''

"This is the first time I have told it since that day, but what happened after was worse for me. My Mama had told me that I must never play with Master Robin again, but one day about a week after Harry died I was walking through the woods alone and came upon him unexpectedly. He tied me to a tree then asked me if I had told on him. I said no, no one knew. He beat my legs with a stick and said perhaps he would kill me too, in case I did tell. Then he said no, he would leave me for the wild animals to eat. He put his handkerchief in my mouth and left me there.''

Anne held her hand tightly and said tearfully, "Poor Liza, how frightened you must have been.''

"When it got dark I was very frightened, but my Mama had worried about me when I did not return and came up to the Abbey and told old Lord Welham of her fears. He got up a search party immediately and although I could not call out to them, they found me at last. Master Robin was sent away to school the next week and I thanked God for it.''

"Does Lord Welham know of this?'' Anne asked.

"Not from my lips, Madame,'' Liza replied. "The story did get out however, for the gamekeeper who tried to save Harry saw Robin standing on the bank and told people of it. Maybe our neighbours heard me tell my mother, I don't know. His lordship loved Master Robin and would hear no ill of him from anyone. The other stories that came back from his school and later from town are common knowledge in the village, and elsewhere for all I know.''

The two girls, engrossed in their conversation, were hardly aware that the pony-trap had turned in at the drive gates. Some way up the drive, where it turned sharply to proceed towards the house, a rabbit bolted across the path and startled the pony. Francis, unused to driving, did the wrong thing, and the trap lurched alarmingly on one wheel before bouncing back to be drawn at a breathtaking pace up the remaining half of the drive by a thoroughly frightened pony.

Lord Welham was extremely relieved to have finished his business with his steward and after sending him with Porter to be given lunch, had wandered out onto the front terrace for a breath of air. He heard the sound of wheels on the drive, and glancing up was privileged to see the whole spectacular incident with the trap. He stood frozen with horror as the pony proceeded at breakneck speed towards him and his horror turned to blinding rage when he saw who was at the reins. The sight of Lord Welham on the terrace acted like a charm on Francis, who exerting all of his energy, managed to bring the pony to a standstill at the bottom of the steps. Lord Welham stepped down and held the pony's head whilst a very frightened Francis dismounted and helped Anne and Liza to alight.

"Liza, Francis, to my library immediately," Lord Welham ordered.

Anne turned toward him. "No. Oh, no," she said hastily. "It was an accident."

Taking no notice of her the two servants entered the house and as a groom came running up to relieve Lord Welham, he took her arm and led her protesting up the steps. Anne had been frightened by the mishap in the trap but she was well aware that Lord Welham was incensed. As she entered the hall she saw the library door shut behind the two miscreants and throwing caution to the winds she said again, "It was no fault of theirs, my lord, it was an accident. If you wish to blame anyone then blame me."

"I do," he said harshly and continued up the staircase still holding her arm. If Anne had only known it Lord Welham had suffered a severe shock when the trap threatened to overturn. For one blinding moment he had seen, in his mind, Anne being thrown out on to the drive. When he perceived that she was still safe his shock had turned to anger as is often the case. Opening the door of her sitting-room he marched her in then turned her to face him. "You do realise you might have been killed," he said angrily. "How dare you flout me and go driving without a groom."

Anne snatched her arm from his hold and said with great

heat, "Flout you, my lord, flout you. To whom did you give this *order* might I ask, certainly not to me I assure you."

"To the stables, Madame. I can only assume you overrode my order. To allow a footman to drive you was foolhardy." "Not so, my lord, Francis was taught to drive by his brother who is head groom to the Squire. But for the chance of a rabbit across the path all would have been well." She took off her bonnet and disregarding Lord Welham walked across the room to lay it on a table. He strode towards her and swung her round to face him. Blazing with anger he said, "Any fool will tell you that a good whipster does not overset a carriage for the sake of a rabbit. Only on your orders would he have been allowed to drive that trap out of the stables."

"I sent him to the stables for it certainly. Therefore he is not to blame, and why you wish to speak to Liza I can have no conception. It does not concern her at all." Anne spoke with a quiet dignity which enraged Lord Welham even more.

"It concerns every member of my staff who allowed you to do this stupid thing," he raged. "From Porter to the head groom."

Anne's temper snapped then and she said in great anger, "How like you to blame everyone, to shout and rage, my lord, and thoroughly frighten people who can not answer you back. This is just in your style."

"I shall do as I please in my own home, Madame, and you do well to remember it. When I give orders I expect them to be obeyed." He marched angrily to the door and turning said, "We will speak of this further when you are not in a temper."

"And you also, my lord," Anne snapped. "Or I shall have nothing further to say." Unable to think of an answer Lord Welham flung the door open and slammed it behind him, giving Anne the satisfaction of having had the last word. She did not go down to luncheon feeling unable to face Lord Welham at present and later in the afternoon rang her bell for Liza. A very subdued and dejected girl entered and Anne was instantly contrite as she remembered that Liza had not wanted her to drive with Francis.

"Oh Liza, I am very sorry to have got you into trouble my dear. Was Lord Welham very angry with you?"

"Yes, Madame," Liza said tearfully. "He said for my mother's sake he would not dismiss me, but had there been anyone else in the house who could have waited on you I would have been reduced to parlourmaid."

"How unkind of him. Did you tell him I made you go?"

"No, Madame," said Liza shocked. "How could I?"

"But you should have. I told him I was to blame. What did he say to Francis?"

"Francis is no longer your personal footman, Madame, he is replaced by George," Liza said quietly. "He is very upset by it, but Porter says it serves him right."

"Oh, how stupid that man is, I told him plainly that I had sent Francis to the stables. Does he never listen."

"Francis told him that he had offered to drive you. He didn't want his lordship to be angry with you, Madame."

"Liza," Anne said guiltily, "You have both been in trouble because of me, I cannot allow it. I shall go to see Lord Welham and tell him so."

"No, Madame, better to stay away until his temper has cooled," Liza said placatingly. Being an intelligent girl she was aware that most of Lord Welham's anger had been born of fear for the girl he loved. Anne, not having the knowledge that Liza had, saw only arrogance in his actions. Disregarding Liza she went to find him and ran him to earth in his gun-room. He was happily employed in cleaning the shotgun that he had been using that morning. Looking up at Anne's entrance he saw the anger in her face, and resolved to control his own temper at all costs, her parting remark to him being fresh in his mind.

In a cold hard voice Anne opened the conversation. "I have already told you, my lord, that I was to blame, both for Francis driving the trap and for Liza accompanying me. It has therefore shocked me greatly to learn that you shouted at Liza and made her cry, but by far worse you have removed Francis from a position of prestige."

"That is quite correct," he said calmly. "Liza informed me that she knew you should not drive without a groom and Francis abused his position by offering to drive you."

"But they only said that to save *me* from your anger," Anne said impatiently.

"Then Liza did not know, and Francis did not offer to drive you. Is that correct?" he said with aggravating calm.

"No, yes, no. Oh don't you see they were trying to help me and for that they are in trouble? How can I bear it when it is my fault," she said pleadingly.

"Perhaps in future you will heed their advice," he answered without looking up.

"Is that why you are punishing them?" Anne said heatedly. "To punish me?"

"No," he said gravely, "Merely to teach you all a salutary lesson."

"I need no lessons from you, my lord," Anne said in a hollow voice. "Your cousin taught me all I need to know about men."

Lord Welham looked at her sharply and said in a voice of reproof, "Anne, there is no need to remind me of that."

"Then you will return Francis to me," she said.

"No," he replied, "I will not."

"And I will not have George," she said instantly. "You may tell him so."

He came to her and took her hands in his. "You do not

understand about running a house like this, my dear. If my orders are not obeyed, soon everything would be in chaos. I am sorry I was angry with you, and in truth it was only fear for your safety that made me so angry.'' He looked at her anxiously but she would not meet his eye.

''But you do not care that I feel responsible for causing two people unhappiness. You do not care enough for that.'' She looked at him with tear-filled eyes, and Oliver Welham made the biggest mistake in his life. Pulling her close to him he said tenderly, ''I care a great deal more than that, Anne. I love you my dear and want to marry you.''

''No! no!'' she cried tearing herself from his grasp. ''How dare you, how dare you say that! It is not true, I don't want to hear it.'' She backed to the door and he took a step towards her saying, ''Anne, please Anne.''

''Leave me alone, don't touch me,'' she screamed, ''I hate you, you are a Rowley like him. I will never marry you, you can't make me, I will never marry anyone; it's terrible, terrible.''

She fled from the room and up the staircase leaving Oliver to curse the fate that had made him declare himself too soon. I have lost her, he thought wistfully, through my own stupidity, I have lost her.

Anne fled to her sitting-room and throwing herself on her sofa wept bitterly. She wanted to go to Nanny but was not allowed to. What could she do? Supposing Nanny died, Lord Welham would have her at his mercy. Perhaps he *could* make her marry him with Nanny out of the way. She remembered how he had picked her up and carried her to her room on the day when Nanny became ill. She had felt powerless and rather afraid on that occasion, realising that there was no one in the house who would dare to go against him. And now, Liza and Francis, her two faithful servants were powerless to help her, afraid, as she was, of their domineering Master. What could she do—there was no one to help her—to whom could she turn? She must escape before it was too late—. She jumped up suddenly and went to her bedroom. In a state bordering on hysteria she searched at the back of her closet and found the clothes that she had arrived in, four months ago. She put them on hastily and taking her small bag put a nightdress, some undergarments, and a hairbrush in it. Luck favoured her as she crept down the back stairs and out of a side door. She passed behind the stables and set off through the home wood in the direction, as far as she was able to ascertain, of Cirencester.

Lord Welham left the gun-room half an hour later and made his way up the stairs to Anne's sitting-room. He had decided that he must try in some way to allay her fears, even if it meant denying his love for her. When he could not find her, he rang the bell. Liza, when she came, was able to tell him nothing of her whereabouts, but whilst Lord Welham went to look in the gardens, she studied the bedroom. Something was wrong, of that she was sure. She quickly noticed the absence of the hairbrush and, noticing also that the door of the closet was ajar, one look was enough to confirm her worst fears. She flew down the staircase and reported to Porter who sent a footman for Lord Welham.

"The clothes she came here in, my lord, and her small bag and hairbrush. All gone," Liza said fearfully.

"Go to her room and build up the fire," Lord Welham said briskly, "Put warm pans in the bed, and Porter . . ."

"Yes, my Lord."

"My horse immediately and John Groom."

Lord Welham's head groom grasped the situation immediately. "She will not have gone towards the lake, my lord, nor taken the main drive I think, therefore she must have passed the stables. Someone may have seen her."

"That's what I hope John. See what you can discover for me."

By the time that Lord Welham was mounted, a very small stable boy had been found who had seen a lady in brown pass behind the stables and go into the wood. Lord Welham set off to follow the trail. He passed along the footpath through the wood and coming out onto clear ground cast around for some indication of Anne's direction. Away to his right he could see the spire of the village church. Not that way he thought, but where will she be making for? She knows no one. He rode up the slope to the top of a small hill and surveyed the countryside. In a great sweep across the skyline were the Cotswolds and to his left hidden from sight lay Cirencester. Of course, Cirencester, Jim Bates. Spurring his horse down the hill he made for the village of Bibury. Ten minutes later with the village in sight he rode towards a small spinney which had a path through it. He thought he had seen a flash of movement through the trees and he was right.

Anne had been walking for an hour and was very tired and very frightened. She had begun to realise that she would not reach Cirencester before the early darkness of February came upon her. When she heard the sound of hoofbeats she knew instantly who it would be and scrambling off the path threw herself into a tangle of bushes and lay still. She heard the horse stop some way up the path, then the sound of feet moving nearer to her hiding-place.

"Come out, Anne," Lord Welham called gently, "I know you are there." She held her breath and heard him moving again. "Come out, child, it will be dark soon and you must come home." He stopped beside the bush and parted the branches. She gave a scream of terror and leapt to her feet.

"Leave me alone, leave me alone," she shouted hysterically, I will not, I will not, you cannot make me."

He moved slowly towards her watching her carefully, but his concentration made him frown, and Anne's fragile nerves snapped at his look of apparent cruelty. She opened her mouth and screamed with terror, then just screamed and screamed. Lord Welham stepped quickly forward and drawing back his hand slapped her stingingly across the cheek. The screams stopped instantly and Anne stood like a frozen statue with her mouth wide open and the print of his hand on her face. Putting both arms around her he drew her close to him and softly stroking her hair spoke to her gently, "I had to slap you, my dear, you were hysterical. I didn't want to hurt you. Tell me you understand, Anne, speak to me, child, tell my you know why I hit you. Only forgive me, little one, you know I would never hurt you. Tell me, Anne, speak to me, speak to me."

At last he felt a long shudder pass through her body and suddenly there were tears on the hand that was stroking her face. He waited until the sobbing had ceased before he turned her face up to him. "Tell me now, Anne, tell me you understand why I hit you."

She looked up at him and said in a whisper, "I understand, my lord, I was screaming. You wanted to stop me."

He held her close for a long moment then said, "Thank God you understand, child."

She moved in his arms and putting her hands on his chest pushed him away. He let her go instantly and was relieved when, after searching her pockets, she said in a small voice, "I have no handkerchief."

Stepping up to her he put one hand under her chin and gently wiped her face, then still holding her chin he said, "I am afraid that I frightened you this afternoon and it was very foolish of me. I had to come and find you to tell you so, and also to take you back in case Mrs. Manning heard that you were gone and became anxious." He saw her face relax at his reassuring words and he continued, "Will you forget what I said, if I promise never to mention it again, and come home with me?" He smiled kindly at her and was rewarded with a half smile in return.

"Perhaps I misunderstood you, my lord."

"Perhaps you did," he said gently.

"I would like to go back, but I am afraid that I can walk no further. I think I have a large blister on my foot." He looked down and was dismayed to see that she was wearing thin house sandals. They were soaked through and the bottom of her dress was mud-stained and wet also.

"I have no carriage, child, only my horse. Do you think you could ride in front of me if I held you on?"

"Not on a horse," she said miserably, "Please, my lord, I can't do it."

"Do you think we might just try once," he asked gently. "If you close your eyes very tight, I will lift you onto the saddle sideways and be up beside you immediately. You can sit on my legs and will not be touching the horse at all. In ten minutes we will be home." He searched her face and saw only misery there. "I know you have the courage, if you will only try," he said soothingly.

Anne looked about her at the dark trees and weighed one fear against the other. "I will try," she said bravely, "but I cannot promise success."

"Good girl," he said encouragingly. She closed her eyes and with his arm about her shoulders to guide her, began to walk back along the path. She could hear the horse as they came close to it, but before she had time to demure he had turned her round and swung her up on the saddle. Panic welled up inside her and she opened her eyes wide but Lord Welham was in the saddle that moment and drew her onto his lap. With one arm tightly around her he said, "Bury your face, child, and think of your nice warm bed."

She turned towards him and put both arms around him and buried her face in his jacket.

Half an hour later, sitting up in bed with a cup of hot soup she said to Liza, "It was very silly of me to run away and I am ashamed of myself. Do you think he will tell Nanny?"

"I shouldn't think so, Madame, for fear of worrying her. Why did you run away, my dear? Was it because of Francis and me?"

"Well, not precisely, Liza. You see when I asked Lord Welham to let me have Francis back he said no. After that he said he loved me and wanted to marry me." She looked at Liza and smiled, "It was so silly really, but it frightened me. I don't know why," she said wonderingly. "I can't remember now."

"I don't suppose you will be wanting to think of marrying at present, Madame, that will be why," Liza said soothingly, "But later on, perhaps much later on, you may well meet someone and fall in love. It's human nature you see." She smiled brightly at Anne and went a little pink.

"Why, Liza," Anne said softly, "I do believe you are in love."

"I am, Madame, with Ned the second groom."

"And are you going to marry him?"

"Not yet awhile, Madame, I'm not ready yet, like you."

Anne sat quietly for a moment then said, "Lord Welham said he did not mean it and I was to forget it. He says I can have Francis back again if I wish." Liza went quietly about her duties, privately thinking that Lord Welham had recovered well from a disastrous start. Her mother would be very interested to hear what had happened this day. Maybe she would tell Ned too, but only if she felt like it.

Anne watched Liza arranging her hair in the glass. "How clever you are with hair, Liza," she said, "This is a new style I think."

"Yes, Madame, for the Spring,." Liza replied, "Today is the first day of Spring."

"So it is and I had forgotten," Anne said with a smile. "I should have known for when I walked with Lord Welham yesterday we found primroses in the wood."

"And soon you will be going to Town for the Season," Liza said brightly.

"Not I, Liza," Anne said, "Lord Welham may go but I shall not."

"Not go, Madame!" Liza said in a disappointed voice.

"No, for there is nothing for me in Town," Anne said getting up and going to the door.

Lord Welham was already at breakfast when Anne entered, but he pulled a chair out for her and poured her coffee.

"Thank you," she said sitting down. Lord Welham observed immediately that she was not her usual self and said cheerfully, "Is something troubling you, Anne?"

"Not exactly," she said glancing at him. "Except that I have disappointed Liza I think. She assumed that I would be going to Town with you in two weeks."

"And you will not?" he asked.

"There is no reason why I should. What is there for me in London?"

"The same thing that is there for me," he said in a level voice. "Company, a few parties and Balls, and the chance to meet our friends."

"I have no friends in London," Anne said stiffly.

"Well, Ivor will be there with his mother, and Freddy and Felicia who are to be married at the end of May. Do you not expect an invitation?"

"I do not wish to go to Town for the Season," Anne said mulishly.

"Then I cannot go either," he replied instantly.

"That is foolish, of course you can go," she said indignantly. "Do not think to make me relent with such tactics, my lord."

"I think nothing of the kind," he said severely, "But I cannot go and leave you alone here."

"I shall not be alone, I shall have Nanny."

"Do you really think that she can take care of you any more, Anne?" he asked gently, "Have you not noticed that since her illness she has become very frail. She does not come down to breakfast now and always retires before the tea-tray comes in."

"Then how can I go and leave her?" Anne said desperately. "She needs me."

"Will you tell her or shall I?"

"Tell her what?"

"That you do not intend to leave her and take advantage of the Season."

Anne pushed her chair back and standing up said, "I will tell her, my lord. I do not wish to go."

"Why, Anne?"

"My reasons are my own. I do not have to tell you everything." With that she swept from the room and went in search of Mrs. Manning.

Nanny was sitting up in bed eating thin bread and butter and drinking tea. Anne was surprised to see how small she looked and thought that Lord Welham was right about her. She had no idea how old Nanny was but knew only that before she became her mother's nurse she had worked for another family for several years. She guessed her to be nearly seventy and wondered why she had never seemed old to her until this moment. Mrs. Manning smiled brightly at Anne and said, "A new hair style, I like it."

"Yes, Liza did it because it is the first day of Spring. I wish I could show you the primroses in the home wood, Nanny. Perhaps I shall pick you a bunch today." She moved restlessly about the room, picking things up and putting them down. Nanny who knew her well waited and at last Anne said defiantly, "I am not going to Town with Lord Welham; he wanted me to tell you." Still Nanny said nothing and after moving around the bed Anne sat down on the edge and taking Nanny's hand said, "They only want me to go so that I may find a husband and I don't want one, Nanny, I don't want to be married again."

"And who's to make you if you do not, I should like to know? It seems to me, Miss Anne, that you are making a great fuss over nothing as usual. Lord Welham has been to Town any number of times and is he married yet?"

"I know he thinks to find me a husband."

"Have you told him you don't wish to be married?"

"He knows," Anne said briefly.

"Then you *are* being foolish," Nanny retorted.

"You don't understand, Nanny," Anne wailed.

"I understand you are getting the figets for nothing. You have never had a come-out, my dear, and it was the one thing your mother wanted for you. She made me promise to plague your papa when the time came, until he asked your Godmother to sponsor you. It was not to be however and now when you have the opportunity to do it in style you refuse. I wash my hands of you, I will say no more." Nanny relapsed into silence.

Anne spoke at last, "There will be so many people I do not know and I am too old for a first season." Still Mrs. Manning did not speak.

"Oh, Nanny, don't you see, there will be people who knew Robin, they will ask about him. What can I say?"

"I think you know, that they will be too well mannered

to do more than mention him," Nanny said softly. "And you will love it, my lamb, to be dressed up and going to dances, you know how you like dancing. I went with your Mama for her come-out and on her first Season she had five offers for her hand, all of which she turned down." She closed her eyes and leant against her pillows.

"Oh Nanny, I have made you tired," Anne said contritely, "I am so sorry."

Nanny opened her eyes and said, "No my dear, it was thinking of your dear Mama made me sad. I would have done anything for her, so good and kind she was and always biddable."

"And I am not," Anne said sadly. "I am a sore trial to you, Nanny."

"That you are not," Nanny said softly, "But I can't deny that when you set your mind on something you will not be swayed. It would have been nice, however, to hear about your doings in Town."

"You want me to go very much, don't you?" Anne said resignedly.

"I want you to have everything of the best," Nanny said, "You've been a good girl to me, my dear."

"I will go then, for your sake and my Mama's, but do not expect me to come back with a husband for that I will not do."

"No, my dear, I don't expect that," Nanny said meekly.

When Anne went down to luncheon Lord Welham was not there, a circumstance that pleased Anne greatly, for she had no desire at present to tell him that she would, after all, be going to Town. Francis when asked could not tell her where Lord Welham might be. Had she asked Porter he could have told her, except that he had been ordered under no circumstances to divulge his whereabouts. She informed Francis that she wished to go for a drive in the grounds in her pony-trap and she wished him to accompany her and not Liza. Her maid was another person she had no wish to meet at present for her greatest desire at the moment was to get right away from the house alone, or as alone as Lord Welham would allow her to be. She stood on the steps a moment later and wondered which way to go. Her eye was taken by the folly on the hill beyond the lake. On enquiring of Ned the groom she was assured that there was a path up which the trap could be driven to reach the folly.

At the top of the hill, having instructed Francis and Ned that she wished to be alone, she climbed the inside staircase and came out on an observation platform at the top. She surveyed the landscape and marvelled at the beauty of it all. Far away beyond the Abbey were the Cotswold Hills, clear against a blue sky with great swathes of pasture land and farm land between. Tiny villages nestled in hollows surrounded by trees. Nearer to the Abbey the land that belonged to Welham, much of it planted out as woods with wide rides running through, was bursting with new life. Beneath her the great lake gleamed in the afternoon sunshine. Suddenly she shivered as she remembered the story of Liza's younger brother drowning whilst Robin watched. Lifting her eyes quickly she focussed her attention on the house and resolutely put Robin from her mind. She had not come up here, to be completely alone, in order that she might think of Robin. Lately she had found it much easier to forget Robin and the horrors of her life with him. Here she was then, almost her old self again, yes, here she was. Could she stay here forever? Could she live on Lord Welham's charity for the rest of her life? The thought filled here with an irrational fear. Both he and Nanny wished her to go to Town and she knew very well why. They wanted her to find another husband, but she did not want a husband. Had she wished to marry again she would have accepted Ivor's kind offer. He was pleasant, intelligent and amusing and she cared for him a great deal. But not as a husband, painful though it had been to tell him so. A smile came to her face at the thought of her dear friend, a confirmed bachelor, contemplating marriage. One might almost call Lord Welham a confirmed bachelor, she supposed, since he had not contemplated marriage either. Her hand, resting on the parapet, tightened painfully on the rough stonework as a memory came back to her. Something that she had forgotten. No, not really forgotten, just put away at the back of her mind where it was so easy to leave disturbing memories. Lord Welham *had* contemplated marriage, to her! She covered her face with her hands as the hot colour rushed to her cheeks. How long ago? Four weeks, no, six weeks since he had told her that he loved her and wished to marry her. The feelings of hysteria that she had felt then came rushing back to her, but she thrust them aside and taking her hands from her face said aloud, "Why did his declaration cause me to panic and run away when Ivor's did not? Am I afraid of Lord Welham—or am I afraid of marriage?" She turned and walked to the other side of the round roof, then came back again and stared at the house. "Lord Welham—does not frighten me now—not now that I know that Robin was not a normal man." She considered her remark and decided that Liza's story of her brother, more than anything else, had convinced her of Robin's abnormality. Marriage then? She was afraid of marriage. But always she came back to Ivor's declaration that she had taken so calmly.

"Logic, Anne," she said aloud. "Think of it logically. Why did you run away at the thought of marriage with Lord Welham? No, not at the thought of marriage with him, but at the thought that he might force you into marriage."

She remembered his strong arms about her and the tender look in his eyes when he said that he loved her. A warm comfortable feeling spread over her and her heart began to beat more strongly. "No, no," she whispered, "It cannot be that, how could it be. I must not love him." In that moment she knew what it was that had made her run from Lord Welham in panic. She was not afraid of him, but of herself. Her own foolish heart that wanted him to love her and wanted to love him in return. "I cannot, I must not," she cried softly. Now she knew why, knew what marriage meant. It meant sharing your husband's bed and she could not do that. Robin had told her after his first night with her, "You are useless," he had said. "No good for any man. You are supposed to enjoy it, my dear, not cringe and cry. What a disappointment you are and how thankful I am that I have Juanita. She at least is a real woman, not a sham hiding behind a pretty face." She knew now that she could not allow herself to love Lord Welham, could not allow herself to marry him and take his love when she had nothing to give in return. She could not risk again the bitterness of loving a man who was giving his love to another and despising her for being less than a woman.

"Very well then," she said, swallowing the bitter lump in her throat, "I shall go to Town, but not to find a husband. Perhaps there I might find a friend, someone who will help me to escape from Welham. It will please Nanny and him and will give me time to think about what I am to do with myself." She descended the stone staircase carefully, concentrating hard on placing her feet carefully on each tread, in order that a painful picture of Lord Welham's tender eyes should not overcome her completely.

Lord Welham had been considerably taken aback at Anne's refusal to go to Town with him. For the past month he had been extremely wary in his dealings with her, being careful at all times not to betray his love for her. He had been thankful that she seemed to to have put the events of that disastrous day in February behind her, seemed almost to have forgotten that it had ever happened. He however had not, and his most painful memory of that day was the horror that she had shown at his mention of his love for her. He was well aware that she had not reacted so violently to Ivor's proposal, and had reluctantly formed the opinion that she held him in strong aversion. His decision to take her to Town therefore and find a suitable husband to take care of her, had been his prime concern from that moment and now he was at a loss to know which way to turn. He had promised Mrs. Manning that Anne would be loved and cherished and since she would not allow him to do so, then he must find her a husband. How now to get her to Town taxed his brain, but he did not despair. He had intended to write to his Aunt Theresa who lived some twenty miles away at Enston Hall, when she *was* at home, which was not often. Lady Radley was the late Earl's youngest sister and only ten years older than Oliver. She was a widow with one son who was safely married. Having always been of a lively disposition she had a wide circle of friends and was always visiting one or the other, or enjoying the delights of the latest and smartest Spa. Oliver knew that she would be at home at this time preparing for her departure to Town to enjoy the Season, and as she had often bemoaned the fate that had denied her the pleasure of a daughter to bring out, he had conceived the idea of placing Anne in her capable hands. Instead of writing however he had set out immediately after breakfast to visit her and tell her everything about Anne.

Aunt Theresa had listened carefully whilst he described Anne's arrival at Welham and showed no surprise at the revelations about Robin. Oliver left out nothing including the broken arm, the thunderstorm and his mother's music-room. Theresa smiled kindly when he confessed his stupidity in declaring himself and at last he came to the reason for his visit.

"After all my plans she refused to go," he finished.

"And you truly wish her to find a husband? How noble of you, Oliver."

"Don't laugh at me, Theresa."

"I am not," she said severely, "I wish to know whether I am being employed to further your cause or someone else's."

"Do you think you could?" Oliver asked interestedly.

"Well, as a woman it is perfectly obvious to me that she is already in love with you. No don't interrupt, but for some reason she is not ready to admit to herself that she is."

"I wish I could believe you."

"Well, you can for I know what I am talking about. I can't tell you why she is like this, but I might be able to help. Of course she wants to go to Town, it is every young girl's dream." She paused for a moment deep in thought, then said, "Ring the bell for me, Oliver, I have a plan."

"What is it?" he said ringing the bell.

"Wait and see," Theresa said irritatingly.

"When her butler came she surprised Oliver by saying, "Tell my maid to pack my bags for two weeks stay at Welham. She has one hour only as I intend to depart soon after luncheon."

When the butler had gone Oliver said, "Coming to Welham, Theresa, but we are going to Town in two weeks."

"Thank you for reminding me, Oliver. I must leave explicit instructions about the packing and delivering of my things to your Town House."

Oliver could get no more from his aunt than, "If I think she is right for you, then you shall have her, Oliver."

The path from the folly joined the drive just before the sharp bend and Ned had to pull up to allow a smart travelling carriage piled high with baggage to go by. There was no sign of Lord Welham however, as it had been decided by Theresa that her visit should be a surprise and so after a hasty luncheon she had packed Oliver off across country a half hour before she departed. Anne instructed Ned to drive straight to the stables so that she could enter by the side door. She hurried up the back stairs to her sitting-room to remove her pelisse and bonnet and tidy her hair. She had no idea who the visitor was except that it was a lady. Sitting on her sofa she tried to compose herself, but when she heard footsteps outside the door she felt terribly nervous.

Lord Welham on returning home and enquiring for Anne had been informed of her whereabouts by Porter. He had left instruction with that gentleman to apprise him of the instant of her arrival home, and this he had done whilst Oliver was greeting his aunt in the hall. "What's to do?" Oliver whispered. "Take me up and introduce me of course," Theresa said impatiently.

"Come in," Anne said to the tap on the door and Lord Welham entered, ushering in the visitor. Anne looked into the kindest brown eyes she had ever encountered since the death of her mother. Soft brown curls, lips curved in a mischievous smile and a figure still good, though slightly plumper than was fashionable, completed the lady standing before her.

"Anne, may I introduce my aunt, Lady Radley. Theresa, Robin's widow, Mrs. Rowley."

Anne curtseyed slightly and holding out her hand said,

"I am pleased to meet you, Lady Radley. Lord Welham has told me about you of course, but I never imagined that you could be so young."

She took Anne's hand in hers and replied, "You have made me feel younger just by saying that, my dear, but would you please call me Theresa as Oliver does. Lady Radley sounds so old." She smiled as she spoke and squeezed Anne's hand.

Anne smiled back and said, "I will of course if you wish it, but won't you sit down."

"But thank you, my dear, if you are sure I am not intruding. Oliver tells me that this is your private sitting-room. I came only to be introduced."

"No, not at all," Anne murmured glancing at Lord Welham, "My lord," she said indicating a seat. She wondered briefly what she could possibly say to this aunt of Lord Welham's and why she had come to stay. She had no need to worry however, as Lady Radley was a chatterer. She was also possessed of great charm, and a sense of humour, which Anne soon discovered.

"I am staying for two weeks only and shall then be travelling to Town with you when you go down. You are going in two weeks are you not, Oliver?"

"Oh yes," he said glancing at Anne.

"That's good because I conceived the notion of travelling with you as it will save me the expense of hiring a courier. You can have no idea how expensive they are now. Martin offered of course," she continued glancing at Oliver and pulling a face. "You don't know my son, Anne, or you too would smile as Oliver is doing now. He is a nip-cheese and will insist on putting up at the most unsuitable Inn just because he has heard that it is cheap. The reason soon becomes obvious of course. Last year he took me to Brighton and you may believe me when I tell you that I had flea-bites all over me when I arrived. I could not go out for a week.''

''Theresa!'' Oliver protested laughingly. ''When you told me that story before it was only three bites you had.''

''Was it?'' she said in mock surprise, ''I made sure it was more.''

Lady Radley was introduced to Nanny at dinner and spoke to her most kindly, which pleased Anne considerably. In fact Lady Radley and Mrs. Manning got on very well together, since Nanny had guessed the reason for Lady Radley's visit. Oliver's aunt had been stringently tested and observed by Nanny and had come out of the examination with full marks. If this was the Lady that Lord Welham intended as Anne's sponsor in Town then Mrs. Manning was quite happy. Lady Radley had the right air of gentility, as Nanny recognised instantly, and it was obvious to her that she mixed in the very best of society.

After dinner when Nanny had retired and Lord Welham had joined the ladies Anne said quietly, ''My lord, I have spoken to Nanny and she has convinced me that it would be wrong of me not to accept your generous offer. I have therefore decided to accompany you to Town after all. However I do not wish for a Come-out Ball or to be presented at Court as I feel my age and state precludes such things.''

''But I . . .''

Lord Welham got no further as Theresa interrupted immediately. ''Had you intended not to go then? Well I am sincerely glad that you have changed your mind, my dear. You can have no conception how entertaining it all is. The quizzes one sees at some of the Balls will send you into whoops and the matchmaking Mama's are positively spellbinding.'' She paused for a moment and then continued, ''I do agree with you about a Come-out Ball, that is not at all necessary, but not to be presented, now that is a mistake. People will think it very odd if you are not you know, and it might start gossip.''

"But at my age," Anne protested.

"Well since everyone will know that you did not have a come-out before you were married that is no problem, my dear." She turned to Oliver, "Who is sponsoring her?''

"As a matter of fact," Oliver said ruefully, "I have this very day sent a letter to your home asking if *you* will.''

"I!" said Theresa in mock surprise. "Oliver you are my favourite nephew." She turned to Anne, "If you will have me my dear, I will be delighted. Oliver knows well how I have always mourned the fact that I had no daughter to present. Oh what fun we shall have. You will have me, Anne, won't you?''

"I shall be happy to do so," Anne replied, then added with a smile, "But I can hardly stand in for your daughter as we look more like sisters.''

"Then sisters we shall be," said Theresa gaily. "Now then, Oliver, I shall want unlimited money as I intend my sister to be the best dressed young Lady in Town this season.''

"I have plenty of dresses and gowns," Anne protested.

"Oh but I wanted to go with you to choose some," Theresa said sadly. "There is nothing nicer than spending someone else's money and the London shops are simply bursting with the most delicious hats, gloves and shoes. Is she to have no more, Oliver?" she said turning a mournful face to him.

"Most certainly she is to have some more," he said laughing. "So do not weep, Theresa." He turned to Anne and said gently, "Do not forget, child, that the dresses you had when you came were made for the winter months. You will need something a great deal lighter for the summer.''

"But so much expense," Anne said guiltily. "I had no idea it would cost so much or I would not have said I would go."

"You will need summer clothes whether you go to Town or not," he said with a smile, "And would you deny my aunt so much innocent pleasure."

Anne looked at Lord Welham, then at Lady Radley. Both smiled at her encouragingly. She stood up and said quietly, "Very well, it shall be as you wish. Will you excuse me now please, I am tired and wish to retire."

When she had gone Theresa said sadly, "Poor little girl, she is like a frightened bird."

"I know it," Oliver said, "But she is also very intelligent, Theresa, so don't underestimate her."

"Do you take me for a fool, Oliver. How could you love her if she was witless? She is so right for you, Oliver, but more important, you are so right for her."

"I thank you, Aunt. You know well how to deflate my self-opinion."

"None better, nephew, since you take after your father. Now there was a stiff-necked man for you. Thank goodness you also have your mother's kind heart, for that little girl needs a world of kindness before she will be completely well again."

Anne sat on the edge of her bed, but did not ring her bell. She smelled conspiracy. Lady Radley's arrival was too pat to be a coincidence. Had he sent for her? She thought that perhaps he had. A tap at her door made her jump and she went to open it. Nanny stood there with a shawl about her shoulders.

"Come in to the fire, Nanny. What are you doing here?" she asked anxiously.

"I told the girl to inform me the instant you came up. Have you told his lordship that you are going to Town?"

"Yes, I have," Anne said shortly.

"Good. I am glad of that. Does he mean Lady Radley to sponsor you?"

"That is his plan, yes," Anne said.

"Then everything will be well. She is a real lady and will take care of you. I can rest easy now."

"Oh Nanny, have you been worrying about me? You must not, for I am well able to take care of myself."

"Well, that's as may be," she replied tartly, "but no daughter of my lovely Lady must be seen in Town with anyone but the best and if she had not been suitable I should have told Lord Welham so to his face."

Anne threw her arms around Mrs. Manning and said with a laugh, "Oh Nanny, I do love you."

SIX

*L*ord *Welham's large travelling carriage pulled up out-*
side his Town House and Anne and Theresa descended.
Porter opened the door to them and Anne gazed around a
large hall with an elegant curving staircase that rose to the
first floor. She was delighted with everything from her bedroom at the back of the house away from the noises of the
street, to the ladies' sitting-room at the front with an excellent view of the park gardens and every fashionable pas-
ser-by.

The next morning found Anne on a tour of all the expensive establishments that enjoyed the patronage of the
very rich. Dresses and gowns of all descriptions were ordered in such quantities that Anne was breathless with
wonder.

"Do I really need so many hats?" she asked bewildered,
as Theresa ordered yet another.

"Is it not to your liking then, my dear?" Theresa said
anxiously. "Well, perhaps you are right. No, Celeste, we
will have the Italian Straw after all."

"Theresa," Anne said laughingly, "I am breathless.
Have you any conception of how much money you have
spent this morning?"

"None at all," Theresa said crisply, "and I had meant

to warn you, my dear, that talking about money is considered extremely vulgar.''

After visiting a few more shops Theresa directed the driver to take them to Lady Stone's house and there followed a round of brief morning calls on Lady Radley's particular friends.

Anne retired to bed early that evening declining Lord Welham's offer of a visit to the Theatre, and awoke refreshed and happy. At breakfast Theresa appeared with a sheaf of letters. All of her acquaintances had written to her, inviting her and her protegée to their Balls, Soirées and Parties. The name of Rowley had also opened other doors.

''Dear Lady Jersey has sent you vouchers for Almacks, Anne, how kind of her,'' Theresa said.

''My head is quite spinning,'' Anne replied happily. ''I have been invited to parties by people that I do not even know and now I have vouchers for Almacks. Nanny told me how important it is to acquire vouchers. Did you request them, Theresa?''

''I expect it was Oliver,'' Theresa said abstractedly, opening another invitation. ''Sally Jersey has always had a tendre for him. Lady Stone is having a literary evening, how delightful. Oliver will be sure to wish to go to that.''

''Why has he never married?'' Anne asked, suddenly serious.

''Who, dear?''

''Lord Welham.''

Lady Radley looked up from her letters and observed a strange look on Anne's previously happy face. ''I am not entirely sure,'' she said carefully, ''I know he offered for Caroline Stewart and was turned down, but he was very young then, no more than nineteen, I believe. His broken heart healed very quickly however and he enjoyed a flirtation with a very pretty widow before going off to Bath with his Mama.''

"And since then there has been no one?"

"Well, as to that I could hardly say no one," Theresa said smiling mischievously, "But ladies are not supposed to talk about such things."

"I wish he was married," Anne said sadly.

"Do you dear, why?" Theresa asked gently.

"Because—I don't know—it would be so much—I don't know." She stood up abruptly. "How foolish I am. It is nothing to me whether he is married or not. Please excuse me, I have some invitations to answer."

Theresa watched her leave the room and wondered why it was that she could not admit a love that was so obviously in her. "It will be something to do with Robin I make no doubt, but how to get round it is something that I do not know."

By the time that luncheon was served several morning callers, with yet more invitations, had brought the happy smile back to Anne's face. Lord Welham returned from his Club bringing Ivor with him for luncheon.

Anne smiled happily and said, "We have so many invitations that I do not know how Theresa will sort them all out."

"Well, some we cannot attend, it will be impossible," Theresa said gaily, "But trust me, my dear, we shall go to all of those that promise to be the most entertaining."

"There goes my mother's Soirée," Ivor said glumly.

"Oh no," Anne said, "Theresa we will not turn down Lady Stone I hope?"

"Of course not, Ivor," Theresa said repovingly to him, "You know well that your Mama is my dearest friend and her Literary Soirées are most interesting. You wish to go do you not, Oliver?"

"If I did not no one would send me copies of their latest books and I would be forced to buy them, which would be most extravagant."

Anne smiled at him knowing that he was joking with them, then said, "Lady Jersey has sent me vouchers for Almacks. I believe I have you to thank for that."

"Good," he replied. "I sent her a most civil letter requesting them."

"That must have surprised her," Ivor said quickly, and turning to Anne added, "It is an age since he has been civil to Sally Jersey."

"It is not necessary to be civil to friends," Oliver replied with a smile.

"I had noticed," Ivor said dryly and turning again to Anne he said, "When you have received permission from the patronesses I mean to claim the first waltz with you."

"Why Ivor how underhand of you!" Oliver said. "I was about to ask the same thing myself."

"You should not be such a slow-top," Ivor said grinning wickedly.

Theresa sat quietly and watched the two friends working their magic on Anne. All traces of the unease that had been there at breakfast were gone as she blossomed under their raillery and became again the pretty young girl that she had been before she met Robin.

One evening a week later found Anne making her début at Almacks. She had spent the previous week in a whirl of Parties, Soirées, Supper parties and even a Breakfast Party thrown by a desperate hostess who could think of no other way of attracting attention to herself. As more and more boxes arrived, all filled with new clothes, Anne resolved to speak to Lord Welham about Theresa's extravagance. When she climbed the wide staircase to Almacks however, dressed in a peach silk ball gown with an overdress of french lace, she forgot extravagance completely. The rooms were small and not terribly elegant but the gowns of the ladies filling the rooms were so beautiful that Anne was pleased to be able to enter with the confidence that came from being equally well dressed. Theresa presented her to the Patronesses and Lady Jersey was very kind to her.

"Will I be allowed to waltz?" Anne asked anxiously. "Do you think I shall remember how to do it?"

"Well, since Ivor is determined to be first with you, I think you will have no trouble. He is considered to be the best dancer in Town you know."

"Is he?" Anne said with interest. "How strange, I find it much easier to dance with Lord Welham."

Theresa, much intrigued by this innocent remark, stored it up to tell Oliver at a later date.

Ivor, true to his word, had some conversation with Lady Jersey when the first waltz was announced and Anne received a regal nod from Lady Jersey when he came over to claim her hand. Although nervous she acquitted herself well and was complimented by her subsequent partners. One of these was the handsome Marquis of Lande, who was pursued as relentlessly as Lord Welham by the matchmaking Mamas. His rather stern expression and obvious high opinion of himself was not to her liking, but she enjoyed the indignant looks that the match-making Mamas gave to see their prize dancing with her for the second time in one week.

Freddy and Felicia joined her after the dance and Felicia said with surprise, "You were dancing with the Marquis again. Do you like him?"

"Not really," Anne said smiling, "But it seems that my Papa taught him when he was up at Oxford and he considers me to be more serious-minded than I really am. He dislikes frivolity."

"What a stuffed-shirt," Freddy said disparagingly, then grinning asked, "Did you see the Mamas glaring at you?"

"How foolish they are," Anne said lightly, then turned

the conversation to the plans for their wedding, which both were most eager to discuss.

Lord Welham took her down to supper and pleased by her happy look said, "I can see you are enjoying yourself."

"Oh I am," Anne replied, "I have had partners for every dance."

"I see you were favoured by Lande again," he said lightly, "Quite a cachet, my dear, after only one week in Town. There will be a few young ladies with broken hearts tonight."

"I can't think why," Anne said, "I found him most boring and odiously top-lofty."

"Really," Lord Welham said with relief, quite forgetting that he had brought her to Town expressedly to find a suitable husband for her.

The Marquis, and several other young gentlemen, became regular partners to Anne at every Ball she attended in the following weeks. It was inevitable that she should run into Lady Drusilla quite often also and that young lady viewed the attentions of the Marquis with obvious interest. Anne found herself feeling quite easy when she encountered Drusilla and was even able to smile at her.

As everyone had expected, except Anne, the Marquis decided to offer for her and being very correct he applied to Lord Welham, whom he considered to be her guardian. Anne was made aware of the fact when Oliver foolishly informed her that he had refused the Marquis' offer, and the ensuing quarrel caused Theresa to flee to her room for sanctuary. Anne's anger and indignation at what she termed his high-handedness could not be abated by his reasonable explanation that she did not wish to marry the Marquis. Inevitably Lord Welham also lost his temper and for several days after the quarrel they did not exchange one word with each other. Anne felt unaccountably miserable during this time and found the parties and balls that she attended strangely flat. Oliver confessed to Theresa that he felt his cause to be completely lost and even when she pointed out Anne's unhappy face to him he refused to be comforted.

"I must find her a husband," he said miserably.

"Nonsense," Theresa replied, "Wait and see."

"I have failed," he insisted, but in spite of his insistence he refused two more offers for Anne from two young gentlemen who believed that her friendly smile was an indication of her partiality for them. Wisely he refrained from telling Anne of their offers and gradually things returned to normal.

The Season proceeded and Anne had her presentation at Court. It had become obvious to polite Society that the Marquis had not prospered and Drusilla's friendly smile became somewhat strained. The approach of May meant that Felicia's marriage was only one week away and promised to be the wedding of the Season. Anne was delighted that her match-making had come to this happy result and forgot the Marquis and Drusilla in planning for the big day.

"Whatever shall I wear, Theresa? I have been to no other wedding but my own," Anne said excitedly.

"You will have a new outfit of course," Theresa said in a matter of fact voice.

"Oh no," Anne said, "I have a great many clothes already, too many in fact."

"But, my dear," Theresa said astonished, "You cannot go to a wedding in something you have worn before."

"No," Anne said with finality. She had that morning opened a bill for two new walking-out dresses that had been sent to her in error. "I have received a bill for two dresses this morning and it is outrageous."

"My dear, it is a mere trifle," Theresa said desperately, "Put it from your mind please."

"Far from putting it from my mind I intend to speak to Lord Welham about it," Anne replied.

Theresa could say nothing that would sway Anne from her purpose. She sought out Lord Welham in the library on his return from a gallop around the Park with Ivor and Freddy. He was still in his riding clothes when Anne found him and the look on her face told him that trouble was imminent.

"I have just received this bill for two dresses," she said firmly. "I am astonished at the price and since Theresa told me at the time that they were very cheap I can only conclude that the other dresses I have been given cost a great deal more. How much money have you spent on my clothes for this come-out?"

He took the bill from her without speaking and glancing at it briefly, put it in his desk. "I have no idea how much the dressmaker's bills have been," he said casually, "That one seems quite reasonable to me."

"How much?" she said firmly, "Do not think to put me off, my lord."

"I told you, I have no idea."

"And if you had you would not tell me?"

"Very likely not."

"I have no desire to be beholden to you."

"So you have told me before, but it does not appear that way to me."

"You pay me an allowance, you feed me and clothe me and it does not appear that I am beholden to you," she said scornfully.

"No, Anne, it does not," he said calmly. "The portion that you brought to your marriage with Robin was no mean one. When your father died you inherited his entire estate. I can only assume that Robin sold it and used the money himself. Therefore the meagre amount that I have spent on dresses for you this Season cannot in anyway repay the debt I owe you.''

''It is not your debt, my lord.''

''It is a Rowley debt, therefore it is mine.''

''How stubborn you are,'' Anne said exasperated.

''I was thinking the same thing of you,'' he said with a smile. ''Can I assume that this peal has been rung over me because of Freddy's wedding?''

''Theresa says that I must have a new outfit,'' she said with a slightly mulish look.

''Well, I am quite sure that Felicia will expect her special friend to be looking her best.''

Anne stared at him for a moment in silence then turning away said, ''Well *I* am quite sure that Felicia will not give me a second thought on her wedding day.''

''Will you then have a new outfit for my sake?'' he said softly, ''It pleases me very much to see you looking at your best.''

She swung round to look at him and surprised a look of tenderness on his face. Feeling a flush rising to her cheeks she said hastily, ''Since everyone persists it seems that I must, my lord,'' and fled from the library.

The wedding was a very grand affair and Anne, resplend-
ent in a new outfit of apple green with blonde french lace, had to admit that Felicia was pleased that she was there. To say that she took first place would be wrong as protocol demanded that the Duchess of Whryle should be first, but Lady Fairfield was in possession of the face that Anne had promoted the friendship between Freddy and her daughter and because of this, no kindness was too much. To be sought out for herself and not because she was a Rowley did much to raise Anne's self-esteem, so that when Lady Drusilla came to her and complimented her on her dress Anne was able to reply coolly and without fear. Indeed

Drusilla was very friendly, and the conversation they had together convinced Anne that all animosity between them was over.

Anne was quite wrong, however, for Drusilla's friendly advances were part of a macabre plot she was hatching to ensure Anne's downfall from favour, both in Society and in Oliver's eyes. The advance of the Season without any sign of an offer from Lord Welham had frightened Drusilla, and uncertain now whether she would ever become the Countess of Welham, as she had confidently assured her friends that she would, she placed all the blame on Anne.

After the excitement of the wedding Anne found things rather flat. She had been used to driving out with Felicia almost every day and at every ball or social gathering that she attended Felicia's friendly smile was waiting for her.

A few days after the wedding Anne sat at luncheon with Theresa discussing that evening's entertainment. They were to attend Mrs. Rowlatt's Musical Soirée, something not to be missed, Oliver had insisted, since Mrs. Rowlatt was a great authority on all things musical. Lord Welham joined the ladies for luncheon and asked Anne if she would step into the library for a word with him when the meal was over.

"I have to go away on business this afternoon and I will be away until tomorrow evening," Oliver told her when they were seated in the library. "I am a little worried that you will be lonely whilst I am away, now that Felicia is no longer here."

Anne was aware of a feeling of regret that he would not be accompanying them to Mrs. Rowlatt's Musical Evening, but she said with a smile, "Theresa and I will manage until you return, my lord."

"But Theresa is visiting her great-aunt tomorrow at Wimbledon, had you forgotten?"

"Well I had, but I can occupy myself here until you

return for dinner. You will be back in time to take me to Almacks, will you not?" Anne said.

"Ivor is to come round to dine with us tomorrow, so if I am delayed he will take you in my stead," he said smiling at her, "But you will be alone all day unless you have an invitation to drive out."

She frowned and said, "There is no one to ask me, except young Lord Proby whose invitation I declined. I shall stay quietly at home and write some letters.

"I am sorry we are all deserting you," he said softly. "Perhaps one of your friends will call round with an invitation however."

"I doubt it," Anne said sadly, "If only Felicia was back. I miss her so much. But perhaps she will not have time to drive out with me now that she is married."

"Of course she will," he said coming to her and taking her hand, "Shall I put off my business until another time, child, and stay here with you?"

She looked up at his face quickly and saw the tenderness she had felt when his hand touched hers. "No, that would be silly," she said pulling her hand from his. "And I do have some pressing letters to write."

With that he had to be content. He left the house that afternoon feeling sure that she would be well taken care of by Porter, to whom he had given the most stringent instructions as to Anne's well-being.

"Shame about Welham isn't it, my dear?" Lord Braye said to his lady at dinner that evening.

"Welham?" Lady Braye said uninterestedly.

"Had to go away on business this morning and won't be back until tomorrow evening."

"Indeed," Lady Braye replied as she selected a plump pigeon and transferred it to her plate.

"Poor Fellow will miss Mrs. Rowlatt's Musical Evening. He was quite looking forward to it," Lord Braye said.

Drusilla pushed her plate away and said softly, "What a pity! Oliver would have liked the new string quartet. I wonder if Lady Radley and Mrs. Rowley will attend?"

"Sure to," Lord Braye said, "Mrs. Rowley is a music lover too."

That evening Drusilla was privileged to overhear another piece of information that interested her greatly. Lady Radley imparted to her friend Mrs. Meridon her intention of travelling to Wimbledon early the next morning to spend the entire day with her aged aunt.

"I expect I shall be fagged out by the time I return, but Oliver has kindly provided me with two outriders so that I shall be quite safe on my journey home."

Drusilla's plan was now complete and promptly at eleven o'clock the next morning she presented herself at the house in St. James' Square. To lend her plan some semblance of respectability she had invited her young brother to accompany her and that young man was only too eager to be drawn into the circle of friends that Drusilla had lately gathered about her.

Porter could find no reason to deny Drusilla although he was aware from Lord Welham's orders that he would not have wished her to visit Mrs. Rowley. Anne's calm reception of the morning caller however relieved his mind somewhat and he left them together.

"Mrs. Rowley I have come with an invitation for you," Drusilla said smiling. "My friends and I are going on a picnic to Hampstead Park and due to Judith Field being indisposed we are one lady short. My brother is waiting outside and will convey us to Hyde Park, where we are to meet, if you are agreeable."

Anne was not acquainted with Miss Field but knew her to be a well brought up young lady. She felt no doubts about joining a party in which Miss Field had been included and replied instantly, ''I shall be glad to come with you for I am sadly moped to be inside on such a fine day. Will your brother mind waiting whilst I change into something more suitable?''

Drusilla thanked the providence that had made her mention Judith Field and said, ''You have all the time in the world, they are not expecting us for another half hour.''

When Anne informed Porter that she was going on a picnic to Hampstead Park with Lady Drusilla and her friends he said, ''I hope Lord Welham will be agreeable to such a scheme, Madame.'' To which Anne answered icily, ''I shall be back long before Lord Welham returns, Porter, so you will not be obliged to tell him yourself.''

When the party of friends were joined at Hyde Park Anne felt some misgivings, for the gentlemen of the party appeared far too bold for her liking and the other two young ladies, who were unknown to her, did not seem to be ladies of quality. She sat in the carriage with Drusilla thankfully, for she was being very kind and sheltering Anne from the remarks of the gentlemen, all of whom were on horseback as was Drusilla's brother.

Some time later Anne watched with displeasure as Sir Miles Penrith attempted sportively to kiss one of the bold young ladies, who had been introduced to her as Miss Kitty Bagshott. Anne found Sir Miles particularly disquieting as he frequently turned his pale, cold, blue eyes on her whilst they ate their picnic luncheon. Lord Milne, Drusilla's brother, was seated beside her and he appeared to be a gentleman although his conversation was practically nonexistent, and he found it difficult to take his eyes from Miss Kitty Bagshott. The other two gentlemen had wandered off and were enjoying a cigarillo some distance away. Tired of finding Sir Miles' eyes constantly on her Anne got up and walked away from the others towards a slight incline that was topped with some large rocks and three tall trees. The view was quite splendid, overlooking farm land and scrub as far as the eye could see. Away to her left were woods and beyond them the chimneys and roof of quite a large house. To her right the ridge on which she was standing ran down into a wooded area that was wild and untrodden.

"Admiring the view, Mrs. Rowley," said a drawling unpleasant voice. Anne turned to find Sir Miles beside her. Due to the large rocks she was unable to see the rest of the party although she could hear their voices.

"The view is very pleasant," Anne said faintly, "But I think it is time we were returning to Town."

"So soon," Sir Miles said placing his hand on the trunk of the tree beside Anne's head, "When we have barely become acquainted." He stared at her with his cold, cruel eyes and smiled mockingly when he saw the flush rise to her cheeks. "To have retained the art of blushing after two years of marriage is an achievement indeed."

"You are not a gentleman, Sir Miles," Anne said with a firmness she was far from feeling. "I will return to the party."

Sir Miles swung round and placed his left hand at the other side of her head. "Widows have always interested me," he said coldly, "They know so much more about the pleasures of love." Anne felt the colour leave her cheeks and knew abject fear again.

"You are afraid," he said with a smile, "Good! Fear always heightens my enjoyment as it did Robin's." He watched her struggling for words and smiled faintly. Drusilla had promised him good sport with Robin's widow.

What Sir Miles did not know, and had not been told by Drusilla, was that Anne was under Lord Welham's patronage. Due to financial difficulties he had been unable to come to Town until two days before, when a wager had made him solvent again. Had he known of Lord Welham's involvement he would have stayed well away from Anne, but in his ignorance he continued to bait her. Placing one hand on the neckline of her dress he pulled sharply and the flimsy muslin tore easily. He put his other hand behind her head and pulling here towards him he kissed her roughly, then drawing his face away from hers he said, "I think the others are about to depart, when they are gone we will go down into the woods and I will show you a few tricks that Robin taught me."

Sheer terror lent Anne a strength she did not know she possessed. Pulling back her fist she punched him full on his nose. The shock, more than the pain, caused him to release her, whereupon she put both hands on his chest and pushed hard. Thrown off-balance by the push he trod on a loose stone and fell to the floor. Turning in desperate panic and expecting no help from Drusilla or her friends, Anne plunged down the slope and into the thick underbrush of the woods to her right.

Sir Miles got to his feet, surveyed the brambles and gorse and decided it was not worth ruining his boots for a little pleasure. "Kitty Bagshott will be willing," he said unconcernedly and returned to the party.

"Why, where is Mrs. Rowley?" Drusilla asked in a brittle voice.

"She ran off," Sir Miles said evenly. "I expect she is making her own way home. She seemed to be frightened of me." He laughed unpleasantly and Drusilla, heady with the success of her plan, said with a gay laugh, "Let her then. Come on everyone, time to go."

The terror that possessed Anne enabled her to plunge through the underbrush regardless of the thorns and prickles that tore at her skin as well as her clothes. The ridge down which she was running fell sharply into a small stream in a gully and Anne, unaware of it, dropped suddenly down and twisted her ankle. The sharp pain made her cry out and as she attempted to climb out of the icy water she twisted her foot again so painfully that for the third time in her life she swooned away.

When Ivor presented himself at St. James' Square at five o'clock he was met by a very worried butler who informed him that Mrs. Rowley had not yet returned from her Picnic Party, nor Lord Welham from the country.

"Such affairs often go on longer than planned," Ivor said placatingly. "With whom did Mrs. Rowley go?"

"Lady Drusilla and her brother, my lord. I suggested to Mrs. Rowley that perhaps his lordship would not care for her to go, but she was adamant."

Ivor was as aware as Oliver that Drusilla's dislike of Anne was a real threat to her. He knew well that Anne's rival was an ingenious and hard-hearted adversary, whose arrogance would carry her well beyond the limits of the morality that society imposed, and a very real fear overcame him.

"I was not aware that they were on friendly terms," he said grimly.

"They seemed very friendly, my lord," Porter replied.

Ivor thought for a moment. "When does Lord Welham return?" he asked at last.

"I expect him at any moment, my lord, if his business has prospered."

"I cannot wait, Porter. If his Lordship should return after I am gone, tell him I am on my way to Lord Braye's house. Where was the picnic held?"

"On Hampstead Park, my lord."

"I shall need my carriage then. Send someone to my house to procure it. I shall return here after I have seen if Lady Drusilla has arrived home."

As Ivor descended the steps of the house he was greatly

relieved to see Oliver's curricle turn into the Square. Wasting no time he climbed up beside his bewildered friend and said, "Lord Braye's house and for God's sake hurry."

Oliver wasted no time either, uttering one word, "Anne!" he turned his curricle and raced out of the Square. Ivor had time only to give him the salient facts before they arrived at Lord Braye's town house. On gaining admittance Oliver asked instantly for Drusilla and refused to move from the hall. Drusilla came gracefully down the staircase and seeing the face of the two gentlemen before her, steeled herself for battle.

"Where is Anne?" Oliver asked harshly.

"I have no idea," she replied coolly.

Oliver took a step towards her, "Take care, Drusilla," he said in a voice of ice. "You took her on a picnic; *you* have returned home, but *she* has not. Where is she?"

"I told you I have no idea. The stupid girl took exception to something that was said to her and ran away. We could not find her so we assumed that she had made her own way home."

"From Hampstead Park? Alone? Think again, Drusilla, it will not do."

"What I have told you is true, you can ask my brother, he was there."

"Fetch him then," Oliver said sharply. He paced about the hall until Lord Milne returned with the footman then turning to that startled young man he said, "Where is Mrs. Rowley?" Charlie looked to his sister for guidance but Drusilla said nothing.

"Well," he said at last, "she ran off so we came back without her."

"Why?" Oliver barked.

"Why what?"

Ivor interposed hurriedly, seeing a deep rage settling

about his friend and fearful of the consequences to Lord Milne.

"Why did she run off?" he asked.

"Miles Penrith said something that upset her I think."

Drusilla drew in a sharp breath of disapproval and Oliver's fragile temper snapped. Three long strides brought him to Drusilla's side and taking her shoulders in his strong hands he shook her roughly. "You allowed Miles Penrith to touch her," he shouted. "You took her out into the country with that perverted rake and left her there." He drew back one hand and slapped Drusilla with all of his strength. The blow knocked her heavily to the floor as Lord Braye, disturbed by the noise, opened his library door. His startled gaze took in his daughter sprawled on the floor with a trickle of blood running from her mouth, Lord Welham standing over her in such a rage that he looked like the devil himself, Lord Stone with a look of anger on his face that Lord Braye had thought never to see on that young man's usually calm countenance and, lastly, his son looking decidedly green and seeming unable to stand without the support of the wall.

"My lord," he said furiously, "what is the meaning of this?"

Lady Braye, also alerted by the noise, came running down the staircase to gather her daughter into her arms. "How dare you!" she cried, "Striking a lady in her own home. You must have lost your reason."

Oliver ignored her and turning to Lord Braye said a little more calmly, "We have been friends for a long time, Lord Braye, and I am sorry that through your daughter's fault that can no longer be." Turning an enraged face to Drusilla he said menacingly, "Did you think that I did not know of your animosity towards Anne? What you hoped to achieve by taking her out with your dubious friends I cannot imagine, for nothing that you can do will stop me from marrying her, but I promise you this; if that hell-raiser has harmed her in anyway I will return here and punish you as you should have been punished long ago by your far too indulgent father.''

''There is no need for you to return, Lord Welham,'' Lord Braye said evenly. ''When I have the full facts of this dreadful business you may safely leave Drusilla's punishment to me.'' He turned his full gaze on his daughter and said, ''To my library, girl.'' Then turning to his son, ''And you, sir.''

Oliver and Ivor did not wait to see Drusilla obey her father's command and ten minutes later they were driving out of town in Ivor's carriage.

Anne had not heard the party leave because she had swooned before they did so. She was also unaware that she had been unconscious for more than an hour, though she was stiff with cold and hurting all over from the ravages of the bushes. The pain in her ankle was so great that the smallest movement was agony. She thought that she might well die if she stayed half lying in the stream. She wondered what time it was and if Oliver might have missed her yet. She wept silent tears for the pain in her and also for her own stupidity in believing that Drusilla meant well by her. For how long she lay in pain and desperation she did not know but the sound of carriage wheels and men's voices roused her from self-pity. He has come back, she thought. He must not find me. I cannot bear it if he finds me. She held herself still and quiet, wishing that her breathing did not sound so loud.

Oliver and Ivor found the picnic spot easily since it was a place that most picnic parties chose. They climbed up the slope to the view-point and it was Oliver who noticed the path torn through the brushwood to their right. They descended carefully and Oliver called out softly, ''Anne,

Anne, where are you, love? Answer me, child, so that I can help you.''

She held her breath and listened. Oliver called again and then she was sure. She tried to call out, but the relief of hearing his voice reduced her to tears. Guided by that sound he found her in a crumpled heap in the gully. He lifted her quickly and called to Ivor, ''Go and fetch a blanket, she is wet through.'' Clambering up the gully he sat with his back to a tree and cradled her in his arms. ''You are safe now, my dear,'' he said gently. ''Only stop crying, love, and all will be well.'' He raised her head gently and kissed her forehead. She looked at him for a moment in silence and then said falteringly, ''I thought you would be angry with me for going with her.'' Her voice shook with the tears she was shedding, ''But you are not angry, are you, my lord?''

''No, Anne, not angry, only thankful that I have found you and sorry that I allowed this to happen to you.''

She shivered with the cold. ''Well, it was my own fault for being so stupid,'' she said slowly, ''and I am sorry that I have caused you so much trouble.''

Oliver held her close and murmured softly, ''Nothing is too much trouble for you, child.''

When Ivor returned with the blanket Oliver wrapped her in it and carried her back to the carriage. A doctor was summoned as soon as they arrived home and Anne was confined to bed for a week with a sprained ankle and a severe cold.

*Sitting up in bed three days later Anne surveyed Lord Wel-*ham with interest. ''Were you not even a little bit angry with me at first,'' she said.

''Not one little bit.''

''How unusual,'' she said wonderingly. ''I had quite made up my mind that you would have lost your temper.''

"To own the truth, I did lose my temper," he said with a smile, "but not with you, with Drusilla."

Her face clouded for a moment and she said, "Did you see her then, that day? Did she tell you about—about—that man?" A faint flush rose to her cheeks as she spoke and she turned her face away from him. He came over to the bed and taking her hand sat down beside her. "I know of Penrith's reputation and I have asked you nothing because I did not want to distress you. Put it from your mind, child." He looked away and said harshly, "I have dealt with that young man and he will trouble no one for a long time."

"Well, I hope you hit him hard," she said surprisingly, "For I tried." He laughed and lifting her hand to his lips kissed her fingers. "Was that how you bruised your hand, child? I did wonder."

"Yes, for he was very ill-mannered and—and—low-minded," she said. She pulled her hand from his and said slowly, "He knew Robin you see, he told me so. Why do people wish to hurt me, my lord, is it some defect in *my* character?"

Lord Welham found himself unable to supply Anne with an answer that would satisfy her. To tell her that cruel people will always find someone weaker than themselves to hurt would be a slight to her character that was so strong in so many ways. He replied at last, "I think, my dear, that you were ill-equipped to enter the world when you did. Having known only love and kindness from those about you, Robin's unkindness and cruelty were totally outside your experience. The fear that you now show to cruel people is to be expected after that. They feed on fear you know. As you grow older you will learn how to fend them off and not be afraid of them. There is no defect in your character that I can see, only courage, independence and fortitude."

"How kind you are," she said with a smile, "You always make me feel better."

"Well you are not better just yet," he replied, "and in order that you may be, I propose to take you to Brighton. Everyone is deserting Town now that the summer is nearly here."

"To Brighton," she said dismayed. "I do not want to go there. They will all be there, all of society, and they will know what has happened to me. I know how stories spread and I do not wish to see any of them or have to answer their incessant questions." She turned her back on him and brushed away the tears that had gathered on her cheeks.

"It is only that I thought that the sea air might be good for you," he said gently. "But if you do not wish to go, well and good. We will remain here although company is somewhat thin."

"I do not wish to go about in company any more," Anne said in a distressed voice.

Nothing that Oliver said would sway her, so he went in search of Theresa to enlist her help. Theresa's visit to Anne was a little more productive. "You see, my dear, I do understand how you feel and I do know how upsetting it is to be talked about. When I was seventeen I fell in love with someone quite unsuitable and was foolish enough to agree to elope with him."

"Oh Theresa, how awful," Anne exclaimed.

"Awful indeed, my dear, but I was quite lost to all sense of propriety. Fortunately for me, Oliver's Papa came after us and brought me back to Town, but not soon enough for all the tattle-mongers who spread the most outrageous stories about it. I was beside myself with grief at my lost love, who I might add is the grossest man now with no trace of charm, besides being penniless. Two days after the elopement Mama insisted that I should go to Lady Swift's Ball.

I wept and cried and declared that I could not face anyone, that I was ruined but Mama insisted. If you do not go there will be so much more for them to talk about, she said, only go and put a brave face on and they will soon find someone else more interesting.''

"Well enough to say," Anne said bitterly.

"Well enough, but true," Theresa replied. "It was dreadful, I make no bones about it, they all stared at me when I entered, but I stared back and my best friend, Alicia, who is Mrs. Meridon now, came over to me and took my hand. After that everything was fine.

"How very good of her," Anne said. "There is no wonder that you are so fond of her."

"Only go to Lady Finchley's Ball, Anne, and all will be well. I shall be with you, and Oliver too. Won't you do this thing for me, my dear?"

Thus importuned Anne was powerless to resist and Friday evening found her at Lady Finchley's Ball, the last big Ball of the Season. Only Oliver's hand on her arm and Theresa's apparent unconcern stopped her from running back down the staircase as all eyes turned at her entrance. In the carriage on the way home Lord Welham said kindly, "What would you like to do next, child?"

"Go back to Welham if you please, my lord," Anne said wearily, "I have a great need to see Nanny again."

SEVEN

*O*ne week later found Anne and Lord Welham comfortably established at Welham Abbey. Anne had taken a tearful farewell of Theresa who intended to spend the summer at Bath.

"But when I return home we shall be forever seeing each other," she said consolingly. "Oliver has invited me for Christmas."

"It will be so strange without you," Anne wailed, "And who will make me laugh when I am feeling miserable?"

"I expect Oliver will try, my dear," Theresa said mischievously, "But he is more likely to send you into a rage."

Anne laughed, then said seriously, "I shall never lose my temper with him again, Theresa, for he has been so kind to me over this last trouble and not once has he reproached me for being so stupid."

"I'll believe it when I see it, my dear," Theresa said kindly.

"But I mean it," Anne said.

"So too does Oliver, whenever he says it," Theresa replied. "And he has been saying it for these last thirty years."

The sad parting from Theresa gave way to the joyful

reunion with Nanny and over the next two days all of the events of the London Season were recounted to her. She marvelled at Anne's new clothes, she laughed at her descriptions of the match-making Mamas and expressed the right amount of incredulous admiration at her conquest of the Marquis. It was from Oliver however that she learned of the picnic party and its consequences.

"Is she then ruined in the eyes of Society?" asked a horrified Mrs. Manning.

"Not so Nanny, only *she* thinks she is. There was a certain amount of gossip because she was seen at Hampstead Park in company with Drusilla's friends and try as we might Ivor and I could think of no way to disguise the face that we had to bring her back wrapped in a blanket. Even by taking the street to the mews, we were unfortunate enough to be spotted by Sir Julian Pryde who is the biggest gossip in Town."

"What's to be done then, my lord?"

"Theresa did a great deal by persuading her to attend Lady Finchley's Ball on Friday and the next evening she went to Lady Stone's card party. It was not easy for her but she carried it off as I knew she would."

"Then all will be mended before next Season," Nanny said thankfully.

"By next Season she will go to Town as the Countess of Welham," he said with confidence.

"I wish I might see it," she said wistfully.

"Trust me, Nanny. She does not deny me now and I am only awaiting the right opportunity to ask her again."

Anne placed a tastefully arranged bowl of flowers on the round table in the hall. "There," she said to herself, "that looks much better I think." She pulled at one of the yellow rosebuds. "Now stay there, you silly thing," she said severely.

"Better do as she says," said an amused voice, "or she will lose her temper with you."

"My lord," she said swinging round with a faint flush on her cheeks. "You were listening to me and now I feel foolish."

"Well, it has stayed in its place as you told it to," he said coming to her. "So why should you feel foolish for talking to it?" He took her hand and smiled down at her. "Two weeks at Welham have restored you to health I think."

"I am quite well, thank you," she said, "and happier here than I was in Town. It is so peaceful."

"Then I am the bearer of sad news, for your peace is to be shattered." He held up a letter. "This is from my brother-in-law George. He and my sister are to descend upon us shortly bringing their two brats with them. There will be no peace then I assure you."

He smiled tenderly at her and she looked away quickly and said, "I look forward to meeting your sister and her children. I was sorry that I did not meet her in Town but Theresa said she was unable to come because the children were unwell. I wonder if she will like me."

He took her other hand in his and said softly, "How can she do any other, my dear?" Looking up at him suddenly she surprised such a loving look that her own heart responded for a brief moment, before the familiar panic overcame her.

Pulling her hands from his she moved restlessly and pulled at the flowers in the vase. "She must be a good mother to give up the Season to nurse her children," she said woodenly.

"You cannot imagine how surprised I was to hear that she was doing so," he said lightly. "She is not usually so careful of them I can assure you. It seems that George insisted, since they were both so very ill. It was scarlet-fever I understand."

She looked at him quickly and then said, "You say nothing kind about your sister, my lord, but I cannot believe that she is so bad. Perhaps it is your dislike of women that makes you judge her so harshly."

She saw a flash of anger in his eyes as he answered. "If someone has told you that I dislike women then they have told you an untruth. I lived with my sister for eighteen years prior to her marriage and learned to my cost that she had neither pity nor tenderness in her."

"And her children are brats, yet you like her husband I think."

"George is a good, kind fellow," he said with a frown.

"And a man, my lord. Always you have a good word for a man. Maybe when the children are grown up you will like them too." She saw the anger rise to his eyes again and said quickly, "I have made you angry and I am sorry, for I told Theresa that I would not fight with you again."

"Why was that?" he asked.

"Why?" She flushed as she remembered and said quickly, "I forget why. Excuse me, my lord, if we are to have visitors I must make arrangements for them."

"There is no need," he said. "The servants know where to put them." He put his hand on her arm and said gently, "Who told you that I dislike women?"

"No one told me. It is an observation that I have made myself. Indeed you dislike anyone who is weaker than you."

"Why, Anne?"

"Why what?"

"Why do you suddenly berate me when we were talking so nicely a moment ago."

"I have not berated you, I . . . ," she hesitated, "I do not know what you mean."

"I have not disliked you since I first met you. I do not dislike Mrs. Manning or my Aunt Theresa, yet you accuse me of disliking all women."

She pulled her arm from his grasp and put the table between them. "Then you should dislike me," she said breathlessly. "I have caused you nothing but trouble since I came here, I have shouted at you and fought you. I have cost you a great deal of money and now your sister is coming to see what sort of woman I am. She will see that I have disrupted your life and will wonder why you have been so patient with me." She brushed the tears away from her eyes and finished wildly, "Do *not* be kind to me and do not look at me like that. I am no good for any man, for Robin told me so."

"Anne, Anne," he said softly, "You cannot make me hate you no matter how you try."

She retreated to the foot of the stairs, then turned and said, "I am no good for you, my lord. I am no good for . . . ," she pressed her hand to her mouth to stifle the sob that arose, "Robin said, no good in bed, I cannot therefore love anyone." She fled up the stairs with a flaming face and turned into her bedroom.

A dull pain filled her inside and tears of misery ran down her face. The desire that she had had to be enfolded in Lord Welham's arms was still with her and she could no longer stifle it. It refused to be put to the back of her mind and she indulged it by fondly remembering how he had held her when he found her at Hampstead Park. She went over the loving words that he had said to her and lingered painfully over the soft touch of his lips on her forehead. "I wish I was dead," she moaned softly, and throwing herself down on the bed, gave way to her sorrow and wept bitterly.

Liza found her weeping Mistress when she came to return the clean laundry. Dropping the bundle on a chair she went to Anne and sat beside her on the bed.

"Tell me what it is, my dear," she crooned softly, "Let me help you, I will make it better."

"No one—can," Anne sobbed, "It—is—me. I am no—good, no—good—and—I hurt so—inside."

"Hush, my love, I will not let you say that. Come now, sit up and dry your tears and then tell me what it is that hurts you."

Liza's soft voice and kind ways at length restored Anne sufficiently to sit up and speak more coherently. Her maid led her to the chair beside the small fire and kneeling before her, held her hand firmly.

"Now you shall tell me what has made you so unhappy. You can tell me anything and no one will ever hear it from me."

Anne saw love and trust in Liza's face and a great desire to unburden herself came to her. "Lord Welham loves me, Liza," she said sadly.

"Well I know it, my dear."

"You know?"

"I have seen the way he looks at you. My Ned looks at me in just such a way."

Anne looked away. "Do you also know that I love him?"

"I have thought so," Liza replied carefully.

"What shall I do, Liza?"

"You must tell him you love him," Liza said deliberately.

"I cannot," Anne said, covering her face with her hands. "Oh I cannot."

"Why?" Liza asked sharply.

"Because he will want to marry me."

"And do you not want that?" Liza asked more gently.

"I can never marry anyone," Anne said desperately.

Liza gently pulled her hands from her face and held them, "Tell me why, my dear."

"When you marry . . . you have to . . . go to bed with your husband. I am no good, Liza."

Liza's fingers tightened on Anne's hands and she said harshly, "Master Robin?"

"He told me," Anne sobbed, "No good in bed he said, no good as a wife for any man."

"If Master Robin told me that one and one makes two I should not believe him," Liza said firmly, "If I may speak plainly, my dear, I think that you have no more idea of what happens between a lady and a man than a maiden lady would have."

"I did not like it, Liza," Anne said faintly.

"And no more would I with Master Robin," Liza replied promptly. "He knew nothing of love or tenderness, but I do, and so does his lordship."

"I dare not risk his happiness however, in case Robin should be right."

Liza regarded her thoughtfully, then picking up the clean linen walked towards the bedroom door. "Ned will not be very pleased about that," she said opening the door.

"Ned? What is it to Ned?"

"Why, Madame, I have told him that I will not marry him until you are happily settled. I cannot leave you until you are."

"But I cannot be sure," Anne cried.

"The only way to be sure is to try it," Liza stated with a smile, and closed the door behind her.

Lord Welham went to great pains not to alarm Anne in any way and forebore to touch her or look at her with love in case it should frighten her again. When the guests arrived he introduced Anne to his sister and brother-in-law and watched his sister carefully in case she should say anything to upset her. Janice however was on her best behaviour and in spite of wondering what a pale wisp of a girl could offer to her brother she spoke kindly to Anne. The two boys were much more demanding however and asked her what games she could play and would she play with them now.

"No she will not, brats," their uncle said reprovingly. "It wants but half an hour to your supper-time and then bed."

"Oh Uncle Oliver," said John, a stout seven-year-old, "Must we go to bed so soon?" He smiled engagingly at his Uncle and Anne was surprised to see a tender look in Lord Welham's eye as he replied, "If you do not go to bed early John, how shall you be up in time to go riding with me in the morning?" John was speechless with pleasure, but his small brother James said, "And me, Uncle Oliver, and me?"

"Well, then I suppose I must take you both."

"You must not plague your uncle so," said their mother, "Or he will not invite you again." She looked at Anne and said, "The usual rooms I suppose."

"Yes," Anne said, "Can I help you with the children?"

"There is no need," Janice said with a smile, "The nurserymaid will attend to them. Come along, George, if I am to be unpacked and changed for dinner you must help me."

At dinner that evening Anne watched Lady Grant and tried to see something of the selfish person that Lord Welham had described to her. There was nothing in Janice's demeanour that made her appear other than a kind and amusing guest. Lord Grant was a delightful man with a wry sense of fun and a light of kindness in his eyes. He spoke equally to Anne and Nanny and even surprised a laugh out of Mrs. Manning with one of his anecdotes about his oldest son. Anne tried to draw Lady Grant out to talk about her children but had no success at all. Catching Lord

Welham's eye upon her after such a venture, she flushed slightly remembering his remarks about his sister and her children.

A week passed in which Anne was forced to own the truth of Lord Welham's observations on his sister's character. She seemed totally wrapped up in her own affairs and her husband and children came second to her in any enterprise that she thought up.

One day as Anne was walking through the rose garden, gathering flowers to decorate the rooms, she became an inadvertent eavesdropper on a conversation between Lord Grant and his lady. The first indication she had that anyone else was about, was the sound of Lady Grant's petulant voice drifting over the high hedge that bounded the garden.

"But what does he see in her George?" said Janice.

Anne was about to step through the arched gap in the hedge when Lord Grant spoke. "I find Mrs. Rowley a very agreeable woman," he said decisively. "She is certainly intelligent and very well-born."

On hearing her name Anne shrank back with her face flaming. How could she now reveal herself? She must go away quickly.

"When I think of her becoming the Countess of Welham in my mother's place I can hardly bear it," Janice said plaintively.

"Well I can *certainly* bear it," George said repressingly, "Especially if it will make Oliver happy."

"But will it, George, will it?" his wife said spitefully. "I understand from Lydia Fanshawe that there was some scandal concerning her and Miles Penrith in Town. How could Oliver put such a woman in my mother's place?"

George stood up slowly and surveyed his wife for a moment and then said in a steely voice, "If I hear you mention Lydia Fanshawe again, Janice, I shall be extremely angry. She is a spiteful gossip-mongering woman and if you associate with her you will get just such a bad name as she has.''

''But, George — — —''

''I have not finished, Janice! Why you should suddenly become worried about your mother's place I do not know as you had no love for her whilst she lived and were continually criticising her to me until I asked you to refrain.''

''You don't understand, George,'' Janice said in a sad voice.

''I understand *you* only too well, Janice,'' he said in a softer voice. ''Please do not do anything to ruin Oliver's chance of happiness or I may forget that I love you.''

Anne heard his footsteps receding down the path and shortly after the softer steps of Lady Grant.

''Why did I not go away?'' she said to herself. ''I did not want to hear that.'' She put her hands up to her burning cheeks. ''I will not think about it. Sir Miles, everyone knows.'' She hurried through the gap and along the path to the garden door. In the hall she put the basket of flowers on the round table. A footman came forward to take them and said, ''Shall I give them to Mrs. Porter, Madame?''

Anne walked past him without speaking and mounted the stairs to her room. Once alone Anne examined her thoughts. Lord Welham was quite right about his sister, she was a spiteful and discontented woman, but more important than that she evidently thought that a marriage was imminent between Lord Welham and Anne. That her husband also thought it, was even more disturbing for George Grant was a kind and intelligent man. A vision of herself as Oliver's wife arose in her mind and a feeling of great peace came over her. She stood up abruptly and banished the vision. ''It is not so, how can they think such a thing,'' she said briskly, ''I do not love him—I do not—I cannot—''. Sitting down again she contemplated her future miserably.

"Oh Liza, I dare not," she whispered, "How I wish I could, but I dare not."

A knock at the door and the entrance of Lord Welham brought a blush to her cheeks.

"Now what can I possibly have done that would cause you to blush at my entrance?"

"Nothing," Anne said quickly, and turned away.

"Would you like me to go away?" he asked gently.

Angry at her own embarrassment Anne replied recklessly, "What I would really like, is to know why your sister and her husband think that we are in danger of becoming married."

"Do they?" Oliver said lightly, mentally cursing his sister for her interfering ways.

"They do."

"How do you know?"

"I hear—, I was unable to avoid—." Anne turned back in confusion. "I was in the rose garden—they were conversing—at the other side of the entrance—I would not help—"

"Eavesdropping, my dear," Oliver said with a smile, sitting casually on her sofa.

"I was not," Anne replied indignantly, "I was about to pass through the entrance when I heard my name mentioned by your sister."

"Unkindly I make no doubt."

"She was certainly not complimentary and made mention of Sir Miles—" Anne paused for a moment, then continued briskly, "It was her reference to my taking her mother's place that concerned me more however."

Oliver's shout of laughter surprised her a little and she said questioningly, "My lord?"

"The very idea that Janice should care about our mother's place, or indeed about our mother is just laughable, my dear."

"Lord Grant was quite angry about it," Anne murmured thoughtfully.

"And so he might be."

"But he did not discount her allegation about—us," Anne said sharply.

"I wish that she was right," Oliver said deliberately and tenderly, feeling that Anne's ability to discuss the subject was hopeful.

She turned abruptly however away and said in a strained voice, "Did you wish to see me for any special reason?"

"I came to bring you good news," he said quietly, "Freddy and Felicia are coming to stay with us. They should arrive some time tomorrow afternoon."

Anne swung round with a smile of pleasure on her face. "And Ivor is coming this evening," she said happily, "Thank you for your news, my lord, there is nothing that could please me more."

Anne was not aware that Porter, who at that moment knocked on her door, was the bearer of something that would make her day complete.

"The package that you have been expecting has arrived, my lord," he said, putting a small parcel in Lord Welham's hand before departing.

Oliver turned the parcel over then looked unexpectedly at Anne. She looked back at him, surprised and mystified by his expression and unable to fathom it. He tore the wrapping paper away and took out a small box, then getting up from the sofa he walked towards her. "I have fulfilled my promise," he said softly and held the box out to her. She took it from him and lifted the lid. Inside, gleaming softly, lay her mother's pearls. She was speechless. Oliver watched her lift them gently from the box and raise them to her lips. She hesitated for a moment and he said in a whisper, "They have been cleaned."

Anne pressed them to her lips with both hands and as

the tears streamed down her face she raised radiant eyes to his. "How can I repay you, my lord, how can I ever repay you?" Then she threw her arms around him and sobbed into his waistcoat. He stroked her hair gently and murmured, "I will think of something, my little love."

On the next day, after luncheon, Lady Grant complained of a splitting head and announced that she would retire to bed if someone would assume control of the boys.

"Their nursemaid will take care of them," Oliver said dryly, casting a look at his sister that plainly doubted her words.

"She has the toothache and is in bed herself," Lady Grant said petulantly.

Oliver grunted expressively and left the room, followed by his brother-in-law and Ivor. Anne was more easily persuaded however and as she had become very fond of the little boys she said kindly, "If you would like me to, Janice, I will take the boys for a walk in the woods and you may rest until your head is better." Lady Grant, though holding Anne in dislike, accepted her offer eagerly and Anne went to find the boys and Francis, whom she felt might be invaluable as a guide.

Lord Welham was informed of the scheme by his small nephews and went in search of Anne, who was putting some stout boots on, in her room. When he suggested that she should remain at home and play a quiet game with them she became slightly indignant. "I am well able to take care of them," she stated grandly.

"I did not say that you were not," Oliver said smiling, "but they are rather a handful and I would not want them to fag you out."

"I am not a delicate hot-house plant, my lord, the day is quite fine and I have promised the boys that they shall climb trees."

"And if one of them should fall?"

"I am taking Francis with me to lead us and to prevent such an accident," Anne replied instantly. "Have I your permission to proceed, my lord?"

Lord Welham studied the obstinate expression on her face and sighed, "I really don't think that I could stop you, could I, child?"

"I doubt it," Anne said pertly and left the room.

Anne, Francis and the two boys left the house by the garden door, passed through the formal gardens at the back of the house and entered the woods on the opposite side of the house to the stables. Anne had not been this way before and had to rely on Francis to lead them to the best trees for climbing. After having conquered no less than three trees the boys asked for something else to do. Anne was at a loss but Francis stepped into the breach.

"At the edge of the woods down there," he said pointing away from the house, "is a rope fastened to a tree. We used to swing on it down the slope and back. It's great fun. Would you like to try it?"

"Oh yes please," said John. "May we do that, Mrs. Rowley?"

"Is it quite safe, Francis?" Anne asked.

"Yes, Madame, the boys from the village still swing on it now."

"Lead on then," Anne said brightly, and set off to follow Francis.

A large tree at the edge of the wood stood at the top of a sharp slope and a stout rope with a knot in it hung from one of the branches. "I want to go first," James said instantly. "No, I am oldest," John said, "I have first go." After settling the argument Francis showed them how to sit on the knot and each boy took his turn.

Lady Grant recovered from her headache and decided to go in search of Anne and the children when she learned from Porter that the gentlemen were discussing the latest scientific treatise in the library. Having received directions from Porter she soon heard the high-pitched shrieks of her two sons and made her way towards them. At the moment that she broke through the trees, Anne, in the act of pushing John off for a final swing, missed her footing and was in danger of plunging down the slope. Francis was standing close beside her ever mindful of the trust put on him by Lord Welham to guard her from danger. As she started to fall he threw both arms around her and dragged her back towards him holding her tightly. Lady Grant took one look at Anne locked in the footman's arms and swelled with indignation.

"So this is the way you comport yourself in front of innocent children is it?" she said angrily. Francis released Anne and stepped back hurriedly.

"Janice," Anne said breathlessly, "I slipped."

Heedlessly Janice continued, "I might have known. Lydia Fanshawe was right after all; you are a hussy."

"No, no . . . ," Anne said, "It was not like that." She put her arm round John who had climbed down from the rope. "I was pushing . . ."

"Take your hands off my child," Janice shouted and running forward she pulled the two boys towards her. "You are not fit to be with them. I shall tell my brother what I have seen here."

"Please don't . . . please," Anne whispered and tears began to spill from her eyes. "It isn't true, you must not . . ."

"I shall leave you alone with your lover," Janice shouted wildly and dragged the reluctant children away.

Anne stood dazed and speechless as Lady Grant and her children disappeared amongst the trees. Francis stepped towards her and said miserably, "Mrs. Rowley I am sorry."

"Leave me alone, leave me alone," Anne wailed. "All of you, leave me alone." She turned and ran along the edge of the wood. Francis set out to follow her but soon lost her when she plunged into the trees.

The three men in the library were startled when two small boys rushed in and ran to their father. James was sobbing loudly and John, very close to tears, said, "Papa you must tell Mama it is not true. She shouted at Mrs. Rowley and made her cry. Francis was only saving her from falling." All three gentlemen looked towards the door where Janice stood, red-faced and trembling. Oliver got to his feet immediately and going to his sister said in a tightly controlled voice, "Where is Anne?"

"I left her in the woods with her footman," she said defensively. "They were cuddling in front of my children."

"They were not, they were not," John said indignantly, "Mrs. Rowley slipped."

"Be silent, John," Lord Grant said sharply. "Take your brother and go up to the nursery."

"She was crying, Papa," James said tearfully.

"Go along with your brother," Lord Grant said firmly and the two boys left the room.

"Will you go after her, Oliver?" George said, "Do you want my help?"

Oliver turned away from his sister and said with barely controlled rage, "She is with Francis; he will take care of her. Do something with your wife, George, before I kill her."

Lord Grant walked over to his wife and lifting his hand slapped her sharply across the face, then taking her arm led her away.

Oliver turned to Ivor and was about to speak when Francis entered the room.

"My lord," he said breathlessly. "She ran into the

woods and I lost her. I thought it best to come and get help, but I can show you which way she went.''

Oliver drew in his breath sharply, but Ivor intervened saying simply, ''You did the best thing, Francis. Lead us to where you last saw Mrs. Rowley.''

The three men came at last to the place where Francis had last seen Anne.

''You say she was running along the edge of the wood but plunged in here,'' Oliver asked.

''Yes, my lord.''

''In order to lose you do you think?''

''She said, leave me alone, my lord,'' Francis said miserably.

Oliver turned slowly and looked back towards the house.

''The last place she would go I think,'' Ivor said.

''I think so too,'' Oliver replied, ''and I don't think she would go too far into the woods; it is rather dark in there.'' He turned again and followed the edge of the woods with his eye. It led down a gentle slope to meet at last, far away, the edge of the lake. At the lake side, looking like a toy house, stood a small wooden pagoda.

''My guess is down there,'' Oliver said decisively, ''But in case I should chance to be wrong I would like you and Francis to search the edge of the woods here.''

''Very well,'' Ivor said, ''but I think you are right and you will find her down there.''

Anne knelt on the floor at the back of the pagoda. Her head was resting on her arms on the padded seat that ran around the inside wall of the little round house. She had stopped crying, but weariness and desperation kept her where she was. She did not hear the footsteps that mounted the steps to the verandah, but the sound of the door swinging open jerked her up and round in one movement.

''It is not true,'' she cried desperately. ''I do not care if she is your sister, it is not true.''

166

"I did not think it was for one moment, my love," Oliver said gently from the doorway.

Anne looked at him perplexed, and then said, "You shall not hurt Francis, I will not let you."

He smiled softly, and walking over to where she was, sat down beside her on the seat. "Was that what worried you, my dear, that I should hurt Francis?" He touched her hair briefly and smiled again encouragingly, "Was it that—or something else?"

"I was afraid that you would think . . . ," she paused for a moment and her brow creased in thought. She started again, "I did not want you to think that I . . . ," she stopped again confused and a soft flush came into her cheeks.

Reaching down Oliver lifted her from the floor and sat her on his lap. He took her face in his hands and said with a smile, "You did not want me to think that you were cuddling Francis, is that right?"

"Yes," she said softly.

"I wonder why?"

She pushed his hands away abruptly and said, "Because it is improper for a lady to cuddle anyone."

He put his arms around her and drew her close, "Like this you mean," he said tenderly. She tried to sit up but he held her tightly and said, "How you do suffer at the hands of the Rowleys, child."

She turned her face up to look at him, "my lord," she said tentatively, "it is most improper."

"But most enjoyable," he said smiling at her. "Do you not think so?"

"If someone came and saw us," she said anxiously.

"I sent Ivor and Francis to search in the woods," he said happily, "It will be an age before they work their way down to here." He felt her body relax against his and taking one arm from around her he put his hand under her

167

chin and said tenderly, "Why did you run away, Anne? You must have known that I would not be angry with *you*."

"I was afraid that you would believe her."

"And would that be so terrible if I did?"

"It would be . . . I don't know . . . You see I thought you would . . .," she stopped, "I can't say it."

"Yes you can," he said softly, "You thought I would . . ."

"Would—would not like me any more," she said in a rush.

"And you would not like that?" he asked gently.

"No," said Anne woefully, "Oh no, my lord."

Bending his head down he kissed her lips, gently at first then more passionately until she pushed him away saying, "I cannot breathe, my lord."

"Do you think you might manage to call me Oliver, now that we are to be married," he said softly.

"Are we?" she said shyly.

"Well, after kissing me like that," he said with a laugh, "If you do not I shall think you a very forward young lady."

"I did not kiss you, you kissed me," she said indignantly.

"Then I was mistaken in thinking that you enjoyed it, was I?" he asked with a smile. She blushed fiery red and turned her head away, but he turned her face towards him again and said softly, "Love me and trust me, Anne, I will make you happy, I promise you." He looked at her with love in his eyes and she looked back at him and said, "You were not mistaken my l . . . Oliver, I did enjoy it." Lord Welham kissed Mrs. Rowley again.

Ivor sat on a fallen tree trunk and smoked a cigarillo. Francis standing restlessly beside him said at last, "Should we not search somewhere else, Lord Stone?" Ivor looked up at him. "I don't think so," he said contentedly, "Lord Welham has been in that pagoda for close on a half hour now. I can think of only one reason for him remaining there." Francis coughed nervously and said, "Yes, my lord."

Two figures walked up the slope towards them, hand in hand. The smaller one, obviously a lady, stopped and looked up at the taller figure beside her. The taller figure, obviously a man, put his arm around her and pulled her close to him, then they continued walking.

Ivor ground out his cigarillo and standing up said, "At last! Come along, Francis, I don't want to be late for tea."

From Fawcett Books

Historical Romance at its Best...

Regency Romances

Available at your bookstore or use this coupon.

____KITTY QUINN, Norma Lee Clark	20310	3.50
____LADY JANE, Norma Lee Clark	20163	2.25
____THE TYNEDALE DAUGHTERS, Norma Lee Clark	50285	1.50
____BIRCHWOOD HALL, Denice Greenlea	20122	2.25
____DISTANT RELATIONS, Denice Greenlea	50300	1.50
____A FRIEND OF THE FAMILY, Denice Greenlea	50227	1.50

FAWCETT MAIL SALES
Dept. TAF, 201 E. 50th St., New York, N.Y. 10022

Please send me the FAWCETT BOOKS I have checked above. I am en-
closing $.........(add 50¢ per copy to cover postage and handling).
Send check or money order—no cash or C.O.D.'s please. Prices and
numbers are subject to change without notice.

Name_____

Address_____

City_____State_____Zip Code_____

Allow at least 4 weeks for delivery.

14   TAF-27